RUTH
A Love Story

Ellen Gunderson Traylor

LIVING BOOKS
Tyndale House Publishers, Inc.
Wheaton, Illinois

Library of Congress Catalog Card Number 86-50535
ISBN 0-8423-5809-9
Copyright 1986 by Ellen Gunderson Traylor
Printed in the United States of America

95   94   93   92

10   9   8   7

To my aunt

GRACE FLINT

A godly woman

Trust in the Lord, and do good;
Dwell in the land and cultivate faithfulness.
Delight yourself in the Lord;
And he will give you the desires of your heart.

PSALM 37:3, 4
A Psalm of David
(Author's paraphrase)

CONTENTS

PROLOGUE

My times are in thy hand. . . .

PSALM 31:15
A Psalm of David

The old woman leaned against the doorpost of Jesse's home, peering quietly into the sunshine from the cottage's dark interior. Her large green eyes, still youthful despite deep creases at the corners, caught a flash of fire where it bounced off a makeshift altar in the front yard.

She watched as a dozen men from the village below joined together in peculiar ceremony, and she listened carefully as the aged one, who had led them, lifted his gaze toward heaven.

Jesse and his father, Obed, stood beside a line of seven young men, all handsome as plain-bred stallions, and strapping as young lions. The venerable one, the prophet who had called this gathering, lifted bloody hands toward the sky. On the small altar pyre rested the broken form of a white pigeon, its lifesource dripping down the kindling and sizzling in the flames.

"These are your sons?" the prophet asked.

"Yes, Samuel," Jesse replied, scanning them with anxious pride.

The woman stuck her head further out the door, trying to catch each syllable of the proceedings.

"Lead the lads before me, one by one," the diviner commanded.

The woman observed, her heart beating like a

bird's, as Samuel, the leading judge in Israel, studied her great-grandsons with discrimination.

First Eliab, the eldest, came forth.

Samuel's face brightened in his presence.

And so it should, the woman privately noted. *He is the prince of Jesse's soul.*

But then a cloud passed over the wise man's countenance, and he shook his head.

Eliab was led away, and Abinadab took his place. But again, Samuel shook his head, and Shammah, the third eldest, came forth.

One by one, down to the seventh, the sons stood before the prophet, and were, one by one, rejected.

A storm in his eye, Samuel turned again to his host and demanded, "Are these all the children you have?"

Jesse glanced at Obed, and the grandfather said nothing, but nodded toward the hills.

"There remains yet the youngest." Jesse shrugged. "But surely. . . . "

Samuel lifted his chin in an insistent stare.

" . . . but, he is tending the sheep . . . , " the father stammered.

"Send for him," the seer commanded. And then rejoining the elders who had journeyed up with him from Bethlehem, he added, "We will not rest until he comes."

Jesse reluctantly exited, and was about to send the seventh son in quest of the boy, when the spectator who stood in the cottage door hailed him.

Waving her walking stick, she beckoned him to the house.

"Let me go, my son," she implored. "I was with the

lad in the hills only moments ago. I know where to find him."

"But, Mother Ruth," Jesse objected, "there is no need. . . . "

"Would you have the prophet wait while someone else does the searching? I can go directly to the boy!" she whispered.

The father, confounded by all that was transpiring, at last heaved a sigh. "All right, Grandmother. But be careful."

The elder woman, who knew the trails about the cottage as well as any shepherd, only winked at him and began the trek up the rock-strewn ravine.

David, she thought, her breath laboring under the hike, *my little David!*

With vision undimmed by many years and with a mind keen despite the ravages of time, she scanned the hillside separating her from the sheepfold. A few hundred feet beyond that, in a meadow which commanded a sweeping view of Canaan, she had last seen the lad.

All morning they had sat together, beneath the shadow of an eastward cliff, as David sang for her and played upon his homemade harp—prayers which she had taught him and which his great-great-grandmother, Naomi, had taught her. And all morning she had recounted to him the tale of her life in Moab, and of the two fine men who had introduced her to the love of God.

Together she and the lad had dreamed of the future, and of Jehovah's purpose for Israel.

"To be part of his timing is the greatest thing in

life," she had exhorted him. "This my two husbands taught me well."

"But, Great-grandmother," the boy had complained, "how shall I ever be more than I am—a mere tender of sheep, a solitary singer . . . ?"

"I cannot answer that," she had acknowledged, caressing his dark curls with a veined hand. "I only know, here in my spirit," she had said, placing a finger to her breast, "I only know that you are a man after God's own heart. And Jehovah has great plans for you."

Ruth steadied herself upon her cane and brought her racing pulse under control. The hike had winded her more than usual, for it had not been a leisurely walk.

When at last she reached the sheepfold, she sat a moment upon its low wall, searching the field below. Soon she would see him, but she let herself rest just a bit.

The rays of afternoon sun slanted in the direction of Jordan and the land of her birth.

She suddenly remembered how Naomi had often stood on the rooftop in Kir-Hareseth, trying to glimpse the Holy Land, and wondering if Jehovah had forgotten her.

"Oh, Mother Naomi," she whispered, "the prophet of God has come calling for David. *The timing of the Lord, and the purpose of Jehovah.* Perhaps it has dawned for us at last."

PART I
Famine

How long wilt thou forget me, O Lord? Forever?
How long wilt thou hide thy face from me?
How long shall I take counsel in my soul,
Having sorrow in my heart daily?

PSALM 13:1, 2
A Psalm of David

CHAPTER
ONE

It seemed she could see him now, his heavy, embroi-
dered mantle drawn over his bent head, and his hands
outstretched toward the distant hills of Judah. He was
not here, she knew. But whenever she came alone to
the rooftop, where he used to say his evening prayers,
her heart resurrected him—and she was free, for the
moment, from her loneliness.

"Yes, my husband," she would whisper, agreeing
with his familiar chants. *"The Lord our God is one
Lord. . . . Remember, O Lord, the children of Abraham, and bless Israel with peace."*

Though it had been three years since his passing,
for Naomi, the memory of Elimelech had not
dimmed. In fact, the widow often wondered at its
vividness, and feared for her own mind. At times she
was certain she heard his footstep on the gallery, or
his voice in the hall. She shared her concerns with no
one. For in truth—were the images to fade, the memories to blur, she would be of all souls most desolate.

And so she clung to illusions. And always, the
visions were too fleeting, just as now the dream
receded into the dusk of the Moabite night, and the
fragile impression of her beloved's whisper was shat-
tered by the sounds of city life. As her eyes traveled
from the mirage of memory, however, she would not
allow them to be troubled with scenes below in the

19

street, or in the alien place to which she was bound.
She would, instead, lift them, as her husband always
had, to the hazy horizon where the sons of promise
dwelt—to Israel where the very breezes were the
"breath of God."

There the sun lingered longest, seeming to regret
its passage beyond the limits of the Holy Land. Here,
in Moab, only a Dead Sea marked the western
boundary, and the land was largely bare and treeless.

Fitting, she had often thought, of the land. *Your
origins were ungodly, your very roots withered in
disgrace.*

The widow permitted her gaze to scan the dry, un-
dulating fields which stretched north toward Ammon
and then Gilead. "Why, husband?" she remembered
asking when they had first left Canaan for this back-
side of wilderness. "Why do we not head north? The
forests of Gilead will refresh us. The pomegranates,
the apricots. . . ."

"Now, Naomi," he had replied, "am I a physician,
to study medicine there, or a shepherd to graze my
sheep in those famous pastures? No, my wife. You
married a potter, and no beggarly one at that!"

And so it had been settled. The famine which had
threatened all Judah had been indiscriminate, not
only destroying the holdings of the grain merchants,
but eventually demolishing the entire economy.
When Elimelech's business was endangered, he
might have borne with austerity. But he could not endure the rivalry which had sprung up between his two
elder brothers, both wealthy landowners and noble-
men of the grain market. When their two empires
had been nearly destroyed, the backlash of financial

stress had driven the family into opposing camps. The feuding had forced a permanent wedge of hatred between the kinsmen and sparked an oppressive rivalry—which they imposed on their neutral brother, Elimelech, nearly devouring the mild-mannered artisan. Hence he had fled to the environs of the great capital of potters: Kir-Hareseth, in Moab.

The very name of the place, "city of pottery," supported Elimelech's trade, as the wealth collected by the inhabitants had been founded upon the marvelous works of wrought clay and sandstone for which the town was famous.

Naomi turned to the rooftop corner where her husband's pottery wheel sat, shrouded now in linen to protect it from the dusty winds which incessantly sifted silt and sand through the house. Often, over the years since his going, she had tiptoed up to the balustrade and lifted the fine cloth off the machine. She had marveled at how quiet it sat, the instrument which the foot of Elimelech had treadled to a soft, spinning *whirr* hours upon hours during his life. Shaking the sand of Moab from the cover, she would drape it once more over the wheel which had provided her little family with sustenance, and she would try to find reason for happiness.

But the wares of Kir-Hareseth, their reds and ochers burnished under glazes, swirled and patterned, painted and etched, only reminded her of the trek from Canaan, and the painted desert along the last border of Israel, the Arnon Gorge.

She had not been so old when they had crossed that final boundary separating her from the land of El Shaddai. But something in the abruptness of the chasm had begun to age her even then, and the years intervening had been wearying, eroding as the Arnon, the "rushing torrent" which sat at the edge of this country.

She remembered, even now, how she had stood amazed at the stony, precipitous plunge which the enormous trench and its intersecting wadis formed. Two miles broad from cliff to cliff, and nearly two thousand feet deep, the rift split the red and yellow sandstone of the Moab plateau. And yet, the Wadi Mojib was only forty yards wide at its base, the Arnon crashing and tumbling through a winding knife-slit of earth.

Perhaps Naomi was too mystical, too prone to symbolic interpretations, but she had never shaken the feeling that crossing this boundary was an omen, and that life for her family would be a downward dive so long as they sojourned in this land.

Elimelech, always more optimistic than his wife, had not seen it this way. True to his name, "God is King," he had insisted that Jehovah was in charge of all things, and that even in their bleakest moments, when they could not perceive God's hand upon their shoulders, he governed the moves of their lives.

Naomi laughed to herself, a cynical, unhappy laugh. She had not been able to see God's hand in her husband's decision, and now, ten years after having left Israel, the hope of Jehovah's guidance was even more remote.

She had followed Elimelech out of duty and obligation, but with little faith. And as she lifted one hand to her veil, drawing it over her head against the cool desert breeze, she felt her cheek's dry skin and ran a finger over the deepening crease alongside her mouth.

"Old . . . ," she whispered bitterly to the shadows. "I am old, my love, and your promise has gone with you to the grave."

A young man lingered in the shadows near the front door of Naomi's house and glanced up at the balustrade which hemmed its roof. It seemed the old woman had gone inside at last, and so he stealthily crept out from the portico and entered the street. One more quick study of the roof assured him that his mother had retired for the evening, and his heart sped.

The lights of Kir-Hareseth's square would burn brightly through this night, and the music and dancing were just beginning. If he hurried he would be able to find his friends before they were lost in the crowd.

He knew that on this festival evening, Naomi would sleep fitfully, rising repeatedly to check his room, and worrying over his absence. But she would never leave the house nor go seeking for him during the rites and revelries of a Moabite god.

If he could only be certain that his elder brother would not come scouting for him, he would have no troubles whatever. But once he found his own companions, and once the wine worked its magic, he would forget Naomi, forget his brother Mahlon—and the haunting presence of Elimelech which brooded over hearth and home.

Chilion could not deny what would transpire tonight in this capital city, this sanctuary of Moab's leading deity, Chemosh. Nor was he pleased with the prospect of the evening's climax. Though he enjoyed the pagan wonders of this country, he was still a Jew and had never shaken the revulsion to which the rites of Moabite worship had given rise. This he considered a weakness on his part, however, and not a fault of the culture to which he had become accustomed. If only he could learn to feel nothing—or even to find pleasure in the cries of horror which would fill the temple square at midnight—he would do well, he reasoned.

Better this than to live in perpetual indignation, as his mother did, or in denial of reality, as other Jews in Kir-Hareseth had managed. Chilion would eventually shake his heritage, he was determined. If he were to live out his life here, he would learn to fit in.

So far, none of his friends knew he was a Jew. Even now, as he ran toward the center of town, toward the increasingly brilliant light and calls of hilarity, he removed his tassled mantle and thrust it behind a wayside bush. He would find it before morning, as he always did, and would have it secure about his shoulders when next Naomi saw him.

And as he ran, he practiced the few words whose accent might betray his background. The Hebrew and Moabite tongues were so closely related, both groups having long ago adopted the ancient language of Canaan, that their likeness extended beyond mere grammar, to idiom, syntax, and even thought. Moabite was, in fact, simply a dialect of Chilion's own language, differing only in trifles, so that a Jew could easily function in Kir-Hareseth without being detected as an outsider.

And who would wish to be an outsider? He
shrugged. Especially not a young man. His head
spun as he moved toward the sounds of liberation,
and toward the street torches under which a thousand
beautiful women would be waiting.

Indeed, of all the wonders of Moab, the women
were the most spectacular! He remembered his
father's warnings to this effect—warnings which had
served only to turn his head in the forbidden direction. "When our forefathers came up from Egypt,"
Elimelech would relate, "the daughters of Moab en-
ticed them, and they did bow down and commit
whoredom before their gods!" He could still see the
potter's gnarled finger as it punctuated each syllable,
and he could feel the storm in the old man's eyes.
"Love mercy and walk humbly before Jehovah!"
Elimelech would always conclude. "For this is all he
requires, and if you do this, you shall prosper!"

A flash of torment filled Chilion's breast at the
memory. He of all sons had loved his father, the
gentle and sincere craftsman who had tried always to
raise him in the hope of Israel. But, for all the admo-
nitions, the old man had died in poverty, his riches
spent on physicians during his prolonged and fatal illness. In fact, Elimelech's last years had been full of
cruelty, as he was driven from his homeland by famine, from his brethren by their soul-rending dissen-
sion, and from the loving approval of Naomi for his
decision to emigrate.

Chilion had observed all this, and had determined
never again to trust the myths of Moses and the
Patriarchs.

"At least Chemosh is a father-god," he reasoned, "as

25

believable a god as Jehovah ever was!" So what if he exacted human blood? At least no famine had ravaged Moab or driven its people from their homes.

Here, indeed, was prosperity—and beauty. Chilion halted before the gate of the square and caught his breath from the run. Smoothing his hair and his most festive garment, he entered the arena of Chemosh worshipers, and his eyes scanned the corners of the compound. In every niche and all along the walls were the "daughters of Moab," against whom Elimelech had spoken.

Their faces were glorious, he noted, with charcoaled eyelids and wanton, wine-red lips. Bangles crowned their foreheads and flashed upon their hips, as they leaned together in seductive whispers.

Did they speak of him? he wondered. *Did they approve?*

Perhaps they found his fair skin and pale locks intriguing; his blue eyes, so unusual in this dark culture, alluring. His looks were the only thing he had ever worried over, in his attempts to deny his heritage. Of the two sons of Elimelech, that he should be the one to recall some lost Mediterranean ancestry was cruel mystery. But, to this point, his handsome Grecian face had only won him a following, and had never been a social stumbling block.

True, he was not a muscular man. Both he and Mahlon bordered on the delicate side. In fact, from their earliest days, Naomi had fretted over them, nursing them through an unusual number of ailments, and even, upon their third birthdays, bestowed on them names indicative of inferior health: Mahlon, "sickly"; and Chilion, "pining."

The young man lifted his chin and stretched to his fullest height. "Mother always was a pessimist," he murmured. "One would almost think she wished the worst for us!"

He spat quickly on the ground at the thought, and made his way through the throng. Soon a cluster of young Moabite men had gathered around him, pleased that he had come out, and eager to show him a heady time.

"See—there she is!" one of them whispered, nudging him and pointing toward a cluster of girls beneath a distant flare.

"Which?" Chilion laughed, willingly taking a swig from the wineskin which moved liberally from hand to hand.

"The one I've told you about! See—is she not a beauty?" the friend replied.

Chilion knew very well that the youth referred to a nameless female he had admired in the marketplace. "It would do you good to meet her!" he had insisted.

But tonight the son of Elimelech was baffled. "They are *all* beautiful! Which do you mean?" he asked with a scowl.

Suddenly, however, he was certain that he knew. "Ah, yes!" he whispered. "But how did you spy her? She only now stepped into the light."

Now the companion was confused. Following Chilion's gaze he saw that it had landed upon a young damsel several feet from the focus of his own attention.

"No, no," he corrected. "That one is a beauty as well. But not for you, my friend. I have seen her about, and always she is too quiet—more than shy—

as though wounded in spirit." Here the young man raised a fist to his breast, indicative of a sad heart. "No, Chilion. You want a lively girl. . . ." And here he took him firmly by the shoulders and turned him toward the targeted lady. " . . . like that!"

So—this was the intended one! How could Chilion have missed her? But her back had been to the men when he entered the group. And only now had she faced the square so that her glory was revealed.

A lump rose to the young Jew's throat, and his head was a little fuzzy. "Her name?" was all he could manage.

"I have heard it is 'Orpah,' " the matchmaker answered, "for her long, white neck." The companion studied Chilion's awestruck countenance and laughed quietly. "Ah—so I have hit the mark?" he teased.

Chilion said nothing, and did not move. But when the willowy vamp in the crimson sari glanced his way, his breath came like a tailor's needle, and the other girl—the quiet one—received not another glance.

CHAPTER
TWO

The quiet girl, the one who had first caught Chilion's attention, watched her Moabite sisters silently. She enjoyed their companionship and admired their vivacity, but wished they had not insisted she come out tonight.

"Oh, Ruth, you must!" they had pleaded when they knocked on her door. "Come!" they had cried, pushing past her and scurrying upstairs to her room. "Let us choose your clothes and do up your hair for the evening. The streets will be full of fun!"

The damsel's eyes raced furtively across the pinnacle of the Chemosh temple and down the broad steps of the altar house. How could anyone know her feelings? Who but she knew what horror had attached itself to her heart early on? Surely not these carefree girls. They had never lost a thing in all their lives.

But, as her name implied, she was a "woman's friend," and would indulge her companions one more time. Compliantly, she had garbed herself for merriment, and would agree to festivity without feeling.

Orpah had drawn near now, and tried to win a smile. "Promise you'll stay all night this year," the tall girl coaxed. "How can I be happy if you are not?"

Ruth studied Orpah's smooth olive face and stroked her cheek with a sisterly hand. "An hour from now you will not think of me at all," she said and winked.

"Why, just see how the men admire you. Before the moon is fully risen, the whole city will be at your feet."

Orpah shook her luxurious mane of coal-black hair, and the little tiara of gold bangles shimmered on her high forehead. "Not true," she demured. "Besides, I wish for you to receive the blessing, and the father-god bestows it only on those who stay the night."

Ruth's throat tightened as she fought memories of the last year she had survived the festival climax. She had been but a little child then, and she had never managed to endure another such event. When younger, she had always been able to convince her parents to take her home early, feigning illness, if necessary, to do so. Since reaching womanhood, she had only to apologize to her friends, or slip out silently before the consummation.

"If I stay, I stay," she said at last, satisfying Orpah without any guarantee. And as the statuesque beauty sidled away, Ruth watched her without envy.

The Moabite desert rang with the sounds of celebration long past the moon's zenith. Mahlon knew he would find his brother in the thick of the revelry, but had not expected to catch him in the heaviest of Chemoshite involvements.

The elder son of Elimelech caught his breath, his eyes burning as he came upon Chilion. The youth's blond hair and good looks had certainly proven advantageous, it appeared, as more than one woman, wine-loosened and love-dazzled, clung to him beneath the city wall.

Shoving them all aside, Chilion reached for the one of his desire, and pressed her back against the stone boundary. A sigh of rapture escaped the woman, and all her sisters giggled with delight, watching as the object of their own fantasies worked his magic on their friend.

One by one they turned to leave, scanning the crowd for lovers of their own, dragging them off to dark niches where they would compete for similar attentions.

Mahlon stood numb at the witness, studing Chilion's consort and cursing the pangs which seethed within his own human nature.

Suddenly, however, zeal raged faster than fleshly pulse, and he dove for the youngster who trampled their heritage, who spat upon the teachings of their father.

With a thud, Chilion's head hit the pavement, and he stared wildly into Mahlon's threatening face. Orpah, stunned by the interruption to her ecstasy, slumped against the wall, trying to avoid the two who tumbled about the edge of the square until a crowd collected nearby.

Chilion's secret would not last the night. Mahlon's invectives exposed him the minute he spoke. "A son of Israel!" he cried, picking his brother up and slinging him across the pavement. "You deny your birthright with such behavior!"

Chilion recovered himself, and spat profanely. "Birthright? The heritage of a dispossessed potter? My father left me nothing!"

"I do not speak of our father!" Mahlon asserted, his fist raised in a clench. "I speak of the heritage of Jehovah, whom you curse at every turn!"

The crowd murmured at this, and Chilion's friends, who had just come to aid him, stopped short, wondering at the meaning of these words.

Chilion, reading their expressions, tried helplessly to explain. It was not a crime to be a Jew in Moab, but to deceive one's companions was unpardonable. With stiff frowns, his friends turned aside, not waiting for whatever weak excuse he might conjure forth.

Looking miserably at his elder brother, Chilion suppressed tears of humiliation and pushed past him through the crowd. Mahlon was left alone to face the female who had seduced Chilion's Israelite heart.

Memories of Elimelech's warnings burned his ears, and he glared at the vamp with contemptuous eyes. Turning on his heel, he spat disdainfully upon the ground and pursued Chilion toward the market gate.

The younger son did not think to retrieve his mantle from behind the wayside bush as he ran home. It would have done no good to do so. Soon enough, Naomi would know the truth of his escapade.

CHAPTER
THREE

It had been approaching midnight when Mahlon had found Chilion. The crowd which had gathered near their scuffle dispersed quickly, making their way toward the temple, for the "hour of visitation" drew nigh.

Ruth, who had watched the brothers' confrontation with more curiosity than most, was well aware of the time, but while she wished to be gone from the square, rushed instead to Orpah's side.

The two girls' fathers were business partners, Ruth's being a fabric-maker, and Orpah's a dye merchant. All their young lives they had been friends. Though Ruth had found herself, over the years, having less and less in common with this companion—she cared for her, nonetheless. And since her growing disapproval of Orpah's ways was still tempered by her culture, she repressed the impulse to moralize.

As Ruth drew the trembling girl close, however, Orpah could sense her reservation.

"I know," the tall one responded. " 'Beware of strangers. . . . ' "

Ruth only smiled.

"Oh," Orpah sighed, pushing back the dark locks which were tousled about her shoulders. "I merely wanted some fun. It seems you cannot understand such things!"

Her haughty face contorted into a pout and Ruth looked away. "The men . . . the ones who fought—did I hear they were Jews?" she asked at last.

"Apparently," Orpah said with a shrug. "No wonder they would not stay the night." And then, raising her eyes to the temple, her face lit. "But, you, Ruth—you *are* staying! Right?"

The quiet one hesitated. "Not this year," she replied, shaking her head. "Chemosh has no blessing for me."

Once outside the temple square, Ruth clung to the shadows and crept along the avenue which led home.

Even now the drums and trumpets of Chemosh's procession could be heard snaking through the desert hills toward town, and Ruth's heart pounded harder with each breath as she tried to shut out the memories which the sounds evoked.

Soon she was running through the dark byways, anxious to reach her door and bolt it behind her. Once in the house, she would bury herself in the quiet of her room and try to dismiss the terror for one more year.

Always before, she had left the annual celebration with plenty of time to spare. Tonight, however, due to her being detained with Orpah, the distance between festival and home was far too great.

The crowd could be heard plainly, already, chanting and calling upon their deity, whose enormous bronze idol was being carried through the streets. Soon the Chemosh procession would enter the temple

compound and be borne up the steep steps to his
throne atop the ziggurat.

Ruth ran until her knees buckled, her heart thun-
dering. Placing a hand against a wall, she stopped,
clutching at the pain in her side.

The chants grew more insistent, louder, though she
was further from them. Tears burned her eyes and
she braced herself for what she knew would follow—
a sudden pall of silence and then the gentle rhythmic
beat of drums, increasing in strength and tempo as a
small child was selected from the throng, and
escorted slowly up the ziggurat steps.

When in plain view of the congregation, he would
be turned about to face them, and a crazed frenzy of
praise and exultation would rush up from the masses
whose bloodlust had been piqued.

Some years, the child chosen for this purpose
would cry out. Sometimes he only stared mute and
wild-eyed at his captors. But always, as he was led
the last few steps toward the altar, which raged with a
pyre of leaping flames, he would struggle and try
vainly to escape.

All this Ruth saw in her mind's eye, as the mania of
the Chemoshite throng filled the desert night. Suddenly, terror shot through her, and she ran blindly for
home.

The door handle jolted beneath her grip and she
tore for her room, not even feeling the steps under
her feet.

Covering her head with her pillow, she shut out the
sounds of the temple and waited for morning.

CHAPTER
FOUR

The familiar aroma of breakfast cooking filled the ample court and gallery of Tebit's home. The man stood at the mezzanine rail watching his wife and her servants prepare the meal, and a smile lit his face.

The day following the "hour of visitation" was always a pleasant one for Tebit, who believed the god of Moab had singled him out for unusual blessings.

After all, he was a weaver, he reasoned, and while most weavers were scorned as among the least of the earth, Tebit was one of the most successful craftsmen in Kir-Hareseth.

His eyes scanned the tapestries suspended along the gallery. Colorful, intricate, any one would bring a pretty price at market. And just this month, the month of Chemosh, he had received so many orders from distant parts of Transjordan that he would be half a year filling them.

Yes, though he had given much to the deity, he had long ago overcome the pain of his loss, and reveled now in the abundance which his sacrifice had won.

Besides, he smiled, did he not still have a wonderful daughter? Chemosh had seen to it that Ruth gave the old man love equal to that of a quiver full of children.

Tebit turned toward the girl's chamber and rapped lightly on the door. He and his wife had seen her at the festival, and though they had lost track of her in the crowd, assumed she stayed the night. He knew she would sleep late, but was anxious now to have her join them for the day.

"Child," he called, "it is morning."

Ruth rose stiffly and tried to shake the horror of the previous evening. Actually she had not slept at all, but had remained in bed, knowing it would be expected today, and not wishing her parents to question that she had indeed stayed for the Chemoshite climax.

"I am coming, Papa," she replied.

She waited until she heard Tebit descend the stairs, and then stepped grimly to the washbasin. Her face in the large brass hand mirror was drawn, making her appear much older than her sixteen years.

A cold splash of water and a vigorous rubbing with a towel brought back the luster and blush to her olive cheeks; and as she pulled a comb through her dark brown hair, she managed to smile at her reflection.

Perhaps, if she used her paints today, she could enliven her complexion and her spirits so no one would guess her heart.

She dipped a finger into the rouge which her mother, Marta, had provided on her fourteenth birthday—the day she officially became a woman—and she ran it over the high cheekbones of her perfectly oval face.

Ruth had always been praised for her large eyes. Today she worked a small amount of charcoal into the lush fringes which framed them and anointed her lips with the oil of red Gilead berries, imported from the northern province.

With a sigh she donned the freshly laundered tunic which her mother's servants always laid out for her, and as it draped her form, reaching nearly to her ankles, she cinched the pale blue fabric into her narrow waist. A longer mirror hung on her bedroom wall, and she stood before it, drawing up her petite height to its fullest and pulling the wide belt of Lebanon green even tighter. Tebit was proud of that accessory, having woven it especially for Ruth, to catch the deep emerald which danced in her eyes.

Myriad small chips of pearl and ivory adorned it, enlivening the blue of her tunic, and as she combed her heavy hair smooth against her head, tying it in a bundle at the nape of her neck, she wove a sprig of juniper through the knot.

Pleased with the reflection in her mirror, top to toe, she ran barefoot for the door, and tried to think of something besides the night.

Tebit's shuttle could already be heard clacking rhythmically in the front hall. His little shop faced the street and actually formed the entryway to Ruth's home.

Marta, just ready to call for breakfast, met Ruth with a nervous glance. The month of Chemosh had been difficult for her, as she tried vainly to see things Tebit's way. She, like Ruth, fought the memories of horror and grief which came with the annual celebration. But she dared not question Tebit's prosperity, or the deity's loving hand.

"How may I help?" Ruth offered quickly, seeing that the table had already been set.

"Call your father," Marta suggested. "He rose early to begin the festival orders and must be very hungry."

The curtain to Tebit's shop doors swayed gently in the sunlit breeze, weaving the light into its already colorful pattern. It, like all wares in the Moabite's collection, was cleverly designed to meet a specific purpose. A blend of coarse and fine threads in a frolicsome mosaic, it caught the shopper's eye and drew passersby to browse through piles of delightful fabric lining the sidewalk.

The warm sun off the street lifted Ruth's spirits as she worked this afternoon in the weavery, taking inventory of the stock and helping customers who entered.

Her mind fell upon the same subject which had moved between gloomier thoughts all night long. She remembered the young man who had fought with Orpah's paramour, and she wondered at the words he had spoken.

Two things held her captive to the memory. First, her feminine heart could not help but be impressed by his daring. Though she did not fully understand the quarrel, she knew he took issue not only with his brother, but with his surroundings. And second, what little she did comprehend of his challenge stirred her strangely, in sympathetic feelings she had never framed in words.

And then, he was an attractive man, one who would have caught her eye under any circumstance.

As she folded a bolt of Phoenician purple, laying it upon the wall rack where it would be easily seen, she did so absently, reliving the sight of him, and wondering if he had noticed her.

Surely not. His dark eyes and quick survey of the square had found only his brother, and with the fleetness of a gazelle he had moved through the court. Displaying an agile strength which belied his slender build, he had won Chilion's attention, the respect of the onlookers, and Ruth's full focus.

Hadn't he torn his coat in the fracas? It seemed she recalled him doing so. She mused over the multi-colored swatches of linen and wool which formed a patchwork on the shop counter, and she played a game with herself, trying to select the one which would best match the maroon of the young man's cloak.

"This one," someone offered.

Jolted from her reverie, Ruth glanced up to find a customer bending over the same collection of samples. He had reached for a piece of deep-wine wool, and he held it now against a wide rip in his mantle.

Ruth's mouth was dry as she tried to speak. "Good-day, sir," she managed. "How may I help you?"

Mahlon smiled kindly, not unaware that the girl trembled in his presence. "It should be obvious how you may help," he replied. "You see—my cloak took a beating last evening, and needs repair. I understand that the owner of this place can work miracles with wool."

"Indeed, my father is an artist," Ruth declared, her eyes still wide at the sudden materialization of her fantasy.

"Tebit is your father?" the customer mused. "Ah, then—you would know what he can do for me. You see, I had an altercation. . . ."

"Yes. . . ." The girl nodded. "I was there."

Mahlon, who was used to seeing lovely ladies on

41

the streets of Moab, was nonetheless intrigued by the one before him, by her soft eyes and quiet voice. *But, of course,* he reminded himself, *this is a Chemoshite—a festival-goer.* And if she had seen the fight, she knew he would have no part of her. Dismissing the initial attraction, he set his mind to the task at hand.

"Well, then." He cleared his throat. "How soon can it be mended?"

As Mahlon removed his cloak and bundled it upon the counter, Ruth grasped at a form of conversation. "Three days, no more," she promised. And then she stammered, "But, you are an Israelite?"

Mahlon stiffened. "If you were present last evening, you know I am."

Ruth perceived his defensiveness and quickly added, "I mean nothing by it. I only thought. . . ."

"Yes?"

"Well, I have heard that your people have a law that no Israelite should ever allow a Gentile ware within his home, or upon his person."

Mahlon was used to the forwardness of Moabite women, but even though this girl spoke forthrightly, it was not with the brazen attitude or ulterior motive which her sisters so often manifested. He sensed a genuine concern on her part—and the concern moved him strangely.

"You speak the truth," he agreed. "Many of my people are so inclined. But it is not a law—only a tradition. . . . Why," he laughed quietly, "those of us who live outside Israel have learned we cannot be so narrow and survive. No, my lady," he assured her, "I am no weaver and your father is not a potter, like the

men of my family. We need one another, you see.
Tebit most likely purchased my father's wares, and I
must rely on the good service of the fabric-maker or
go about in rags."

Ruth smiled broadly and Mahlon was struck by the
glints of green within her eyes. "There is much I
would like to know about your culture," she said.
"The God of Israel is so unlike my own. So . . . far
away. . . . "

Mahlon studied her intently, sensing the longing in
her voice.

"Not so far, my lady. He is really as close to you as
I am this moment."

CHAPTER
FIVE

After the death of Elimelech, Mahlon had purchased his own potting wheel. He knew Naomi wished to preserve the old one as she preserved her husband's memory, and so he never removed it from the rooftop where the old man had spent his working hours.

The younger potter preferred to ply his trade at the front door, where passersby might appreciate the craft, and there he sat this afternoon, forming a vessel which would someday be used at the water well.

There were countless potters in Kir-Hareseth, each with his own level of skill as well as peculiar variations on the popular styles of the day. Elimelech had been one of the finest artisans in this city, bringing in a good livelihood for his family. Had it not been for the inordinate expenses incurred during his long illness, the two sons and Naomi would have enjoyed a handsome inheritance. As it was, nearly all the reserves had been depleted as doctors tried to cure the tumor which had sapped the Israelite's life.

Since then, the estate consisted only of the accumulated inventory of Elimelech's industrious years, a small plot of land, and a village dwelling left behind in Judah. Even the house in Kir-Hareseth had been mortgaged to fend off creditors.

Mahlon and Chilion had tried to revive the family

fortunes. But they were not so well known as their father, and their apprenticeship to his craft had been cut short by his demise.

Slowly they were replenishing the coffers, but much too slowly for peace of mind.

Mahlon lifted his eyes to the city walls and thought on the land of his nativity. He had been quite small, only eight years old, when his father had brought the family forth from Bethlehem Ephratah. But he still remembered his home country well, and what he recalled made him lonely for the rolling hills and small white village.

As a child, he had often dreamed of being a sheep herder, a profession very common around Bethlehem. The occupation appealed to him, for it represented the quietest of lives, close to nature. And though he knew he would most likely grow up a potter, he often spoke of the hills and the creatures of the field with fondness.

Perhaps, indeed, Elimelech would have allowed him to follow such a dream. The parcel of land which Mahlon and Chilion had inherited lay in shepherd country. The father had purchased it early on, especially for the eldest son.

But, now he would never know how things might have turned out. Uprooted and moved to Moab, he had never questioned his apprenticeship to the potting craft.

He and his younger brother had not been privileged to celebrate Bar Mitzvah in a congregation. Only before a small party of Kir-Hareseth Jews had they been ushered into manhood. But that day had been a momentous occasion for Mahlon, affirming to him his sonship in Israel, despite his involuntary exile.

For Chilion it had been a joyful event, as well. But the elder brother shuddered as he thought on the direction in which the youth was now headed. His foot raced the treadle and the wet clay spun slick and fast beneath his nimble fingers.

Mahlon had not shown Naomi the torn cloak this morning. He had, in fact, not spoken with her or his brother since rising. For all he knew the younger was still abed. Naomi had kept close in the kitchen since well before dawn, in the typically silent mood she donned when worry pressed her mind.

Mahlon was glad just now for the solitude. Not that he was alone. The street was full of life. But no customers troubled him this moment, and he preferred to contemplate the morning's encounter.

Thoughts of the girl at the weavery danced before him on the potting spindle, and his hands playfully sculpted her feminine shape into the maleable clay.

What would his mother say if she knew he dwelt on a Moabite woman? Quickly he lifted his fist and drove it into the warm substance, drawing the clay off the wheel and rolling it into a neat ball.

Still the young lady peered at him from the mass, ready to be called forth with a move of his artistic fingers.

His fantasy was short-lived as he heard Naomi's footstep on the threshold. Turning, he greeted her with a concerned face.

"Good-day, Mother," he said smiling. "You have been very quiet this afternoon."

The old woman studied her son sadly. "You work

too hard, Mahlon. Hours out here in the sun. You will be exhausted by evening."

The potter stopped the treadle and dried his hands on his stained apron. Reaching for his mother's arm, he drew her close and kissed her on the cheek. "A little cold water," he said as he winked, "and a moment at your side will whisk me through the day."

"Sit in the shade," she laughed, pointing to the small cluster of palms across the road. "I will bring you something better than water."

Mahlon studied her sudden vigor as she scurried back into the house, and he walked to the palm patch, wiping his brow with his sleeve. He had barely rested his back against one of the spiny trunks when Naomi returned, bearing a small pitcher of cold mint tea.

"Here," she offered, pouring a little into an earthenware mug. "This was your father's favorite brew."

"I know," Mahlon whispered, taking the gift and smiling at her gently.

Naomi poured her own cup and rested with him in the shadows.

Almost as soon as the heaviness had gone, however, it returned. The mother's eyes rose to Chilion's bedroom window, and a tight line drew back the corners of her mouth.

"Did you ever find him?" she inquired.

Mahlon set the cup upon the grass and ran his fingers over the cold lip. "I did," he replied.

Hesitant to ask more, Naomi only peered at her son with quiet pensiveness. "I believe he is in his room," she said. "Is he afraid to come out?"

"Most likely," Mahlon confirmed. "He and I had an unpleasant exchange last night."

The mother feared to hear the report, but proceeded with her inquisition. "Did you find him with a woman again?" she asked. "A Moabite?"

Mahlon sighed and flicked the dust from the hem of his robe. "Why do you trouble yourself with such matters?" he rebuked her. "Chilion is of age now."

Naomi's eyes misted. "What should you expect of me?" she objected. "Tell me what you found. It cannot be worse than my imaginings."

The young Jew withdrew into a private silence. "Perhaps . . . just perhaps not all Moabite women are beyond redemption," he whispered.

"What?" Naomi cried.

"Yes, Mother. Chilion was in the thick of folly when I came upon him," Mahlon replied, straightening his shoulders. "I tried to correct him, but his heart is far from me."

The matron rose and smoothed her long tunic. Her head was bent with sorrow as she placed a beseeching hand on her son's shoulder. "Just promise me that *you* will not forget your father's ways," she pleaded.

Then, heading for her kitchen work again, she walked away, glancing discreetly toward the upper story window.

Mahlon noticed a covert flutter of Chilion's curtain, and knew they had been observed.

CHAPTER
SIX

Orpah sat on the low cedar bench of Naomi's court, snuggled close in Chilion's embrace, and tried to relax. She had, at his suggestion, worn a pale yellow gown rather than her red one. "Mother will be hard put to welcome you as it is," he had warned. "Don't wear anything which will offend her."

The girl's furtive gaze shot to the kitchen arch where she was certain she saw the old woman peering out once more.

"Perhaps I should not have come," she whispered.

"Nonsense," Chilion cooed, drawing her closer. "Mother will get used to the idea in time. She will have to, if you are to be my bride."

Orpah giggled anxiously and pulled away.

"I don't know." She shook her head. "I fear we will have more than your mother to overcome."

Chilion knew she referred to her parents, who took none too kindly to her wedding an unmoneyed Jew. The fathers of Moab were not against giving their daughters to Israelite men—provided they were well situated financially. Many such unions were, indeed, arranged across the border of the two countries, especially with Hebrews of less scrupulous taste.

But—to give one's daughter to a *poor* man, Jew or Gentile, drew the censure of the Moab fraternity.

"Do not think such things," Chilion said with a

sigh. "Your father let you come for dinner tonight. He will see; I am proving myself. Only today Mahlon and I received an order for our wares from a town in Edom. I will have a fine price for my bride!"

From beyond the curtain which designated Naomi's work space, the old woman caught the gist of the couple's conversation. Not without effort, however.

Mahlon came upon her, down the back stairs, as she leaned precariously close to the archway veil, her ladle held tight in one fist, and her apron drawn up to the corner of one eye, as though she stopped a tear.

"Mother!" he teased. "Come away from there. You must learn to release the lad, or you will smother him!"

Naomi jolted fitfully, and hurried to her boiling pot.

"Tears?" Mahlon chided, taking her aside and dabbing her cheek with his finger.

"No—only the onions . . . , " Naomi hedged, pointing to her cutting board. "You know how they affect me."

Mahlon smiled, but behind his eyes was a sympathy only a devoted Israelite could feel. Stepping to the curtain, he too studied the lovers in the court, and muttered beneath his breath.

For a moment, however, he let himself imagine what it would be like to sit upon that bench beside the weaver's daughter, and he could say nothing against his brother.

Naomi was mumbling something in the background, and he turned about to catch her words.

". . . so would my father have said," she concluded.

"Your father? What would he say?" Mahlon asked.

"I was recalling that when I was a girl my father would never lightly allow a Gentile in the house. And were it necessary to entertain one, the stranger would not be left alone in any room, lest the place be utterly defiled. So would he have seen it."

With this, Naomi sipped a spoonful of her hot soup and nodded, self-satisfied at the taste.

Mahlon stirred restlessly and wondered if he should stay in the kitchen or join Chilion.

"Perhaps," he replied. "But what would *my* father have said? He never closed the door to anyone. And his home was a sanctuary of the Law!"

With this he entered the court and drew the curtain shut behind him.

Mahlon rose early the morning following Orpah's introduction to the family. It was three days since the Chemosh festival and he knew his cloak would be ready at the weavery.

As he headed down the broad avenue which led past the finest shops in town, he ran his fingers through his shock of dark hair and smoothed his short-cropped beard. His eager tread turned to a gingerly step as he approached Tebit's door, and a peculiar flutter in his stomach warned him to slow down. His pulse racing, he paused outside the entryway and peered in.

The young woman stood, her hands on her hips, behind a stack of new fabric bolts as she contemplated the best place to display them.

"The shelves or the street?" her glances seemed to ask.

Mahlon, enraptured once more with the emerald

glow of her eyes, stammered almost without thinking, "Oh—the shelves . . . of course."

Ruth, unaware of his presence, looked up in surprise, and seeing Mahlon, took a quick breath.

The handsome Israelite entered the store and bent over the bolts. "Let me place them for you," he offered. "Stack them in my arms."

Ruth layered several of the heavy spindles onto his outstretched hands, and he began arranging them neatly on the thick pine planks which Tebit had composed along the foyer's back wall.

The girl watched, amused and flattered, but at last inquired, "Why the shelves and not the street?"

Mahlon positioned the last bolt and turned to her, rubbing his hands nervously on his tunic. "Why, if they are in the street, they will do well," he explained, "but if they are in the shop . . . near you . . . they will show to best advantage." Glancing at the floor, he paused and declared, "Even goat's hair would shine if you stood beside it!"

The Moabitess smiled, a blush rising to her face. Quickly she left the room, returning with Mahlon's cloak, freshly fullered and pressed with her mother's smoothing irons.

She showed him the repair her father had worked on the unsightly tear, and the potter inspected it closely. Lifting it up to the sunlight which entered the door, he sighed in amazement.

"How does he do it?" he marveled. "One would hardly know it had suffered damage."

"I am happy you are pleased." Ruth beamed.

As Mahlon opened the small bag which hung from

his belt, he brought forth twice the price the weavery would have charged.

"For a splendid job," he explained, "a man deserves double honor."

Ruth took the coins, wide-eyed. "You are truly generous," she said.

The Israelite watched her place the money in a small brass box beneath the counter, and his heart raced again. "Few men are open-handed without thought to their own gain," he admitted. "I would be even more pleased with today's transaction if I might come calling now and then."

Ruth interpreted the request easily and glanced shyly at the table between them.

"Have you a suitor already?" Mahlon whispered. "Say that you do not."

The young woman shook her head. "But—sir, I am a daughter of Chemosh."

"In truth?" he asked, a twinkle in his eye. "I think not. Your heart left Chemosh long ago."

CHAPTER
SEVEN

The broad wall of Kir-Hareseth afforded space for several folk to walk abreast along its top. And it was a convenient route for those who wished to cross town while avoiding the winding, narrow streets below.

In the evening, however, it was nearly vacant of pedestrians, the citizens staying close to home when the sun went down. The only ones who might be seen along its summit were the night guards, or an occasional couple dallying in the romance of the desert sunset.

Mahlon walked there tonight with Ruth, as he had become accustomed to doing over the past few weeks. Her small hand in his was warm and comforting and his need to love and be loved rewarded whenever she let him hold her.

The courtships of virgins were not so lengthy or involved in Moab as in Israel. For this he was grateful, though he did bring tradition to the relationship. He would not have seen Ruth, had her father not consented.

At first Tebit had not considered him suitable marriage material for his daughter. Only since Mahlon's fortunes had improved, through the windfall of an extensive Edomite order for pottery, had the man allowed him to call on the girl. Before that time, he

had firmly denied the opportunity, despite Mahlon's
show of generosity in paying for the cloak, and despite Ruth's repeated imploring.

"I am no governor in Moab," the father had objected, and then quoting a proverb, had declared,
"but 'even a weaver is master in his own home'!"

The courtship, therefore, had been strained from
the beginning. But when Mahlon had Ruth to himself, he forgot the obstacles and his heart soared.

Tonight the girl paused along an embattlement and
turned her gaze toward the city square. To the side of
the Chemoshite temple stood the headquarters of
Moab's king. The palace was secure not only due to
Kir-Hareseth's town walls, but because it was surrounded by a great man-made chasm, filled with saw-
toothed boulders brought across miles from the Dead
Sea lava beds.

A very narrow bridge, suspended above this, was
the sole approach to the castle, and had often been
the scene of defeat for Moab's enemies, the treacher-
ous rocks below being the demise of many a toppled
soldier.

Near the palace, the gold-leaf apex of the temple
glistened fire-red in the lingering sun. Legends of
fallen warriors abounded, and Ruth almost felt she
could hear the lads' cries—voices which echoed
through the years separating her from the witness of
her own brother's death. Trembling, she closed her
eyes and waited for the memory to subside.

This was not the first time Mahlon had perceived a
sudden sadness in his lady. Tonight he would press
her for an explanation.

"Whom do you think on but me?" he whispered,

lifting her chin with his fingers. Her eyes were filled with shimmering tears, and one spilled over, splashing onto his hand.

"Oh, Mahlon," she cried, her voice broken, "do not ask. I cannot bear to speak of it. I have never spoken of it to a living soul."

Her lover brooded over her with a persistent sigh. "Perhaps that, more than anything, is where the trouble lies," he said. "You must share your burden with one who cares."

Ruth turned from him coldly, setting her shoulders in a square. "There is no one who cares for this," she insisted. "Even those who are closest to me, who knew it all and saw it all—my friends, my family— they care nothing for this."

Mahlon listened patiently, groping for a way to reach her. Perhaps it was that very patience and that silence which freed her, at last, to divulge her pain. For suddenly, she wheeled about, clinging feverishly to the kind companion.

"He was so small, Mahlon. So young! They forced him to pass through the fire. My baby brother! My little Pekah!"

Mahlon was stunned by the revelation. "You had a little brother? And he was offered on the altar of Chemosh?"

Ruth shuddered and lifted her hands to her face.

"Why, my lady, have you kept this close? Such a hideous memory to bear alone!"

The young woman shook her head helplessly. "A daughter of Chemosh must not question the will of the deity. I am an unfaithful servant when I do so."

Mahlon bristled. "What bondage is this?" he

demanded. "Not only does your god exact the lives of innocent children, but he denies your right to question such horror? My lady—this is against all reason and all faith!"

Ruth trembled in his embrace and the tears began to flow freely—tears of unresolved grief and anger.

"Tell me of him," Mahlon urged her. "You were very close?"

The girl was nearly convulsant as she let the remembrances flood through her, unhampered by fear of censure.

"He was only five years old, when I was eight," she said, weeping. "Dark of eye and golden-skinned. We used to play in the groves along the wall, and in the park which fronts the weavery. Pekah and I needed no other playmates, though all the children loved him as their own."

Fresh tears rose on the tide of hatred she had never expressed. "Why do they not remember him? My father thinks of him only as the one whose death brought blessing to our home. Blessing, Mahlon! In the tragic loss of a child!"

Suddenly Ruth drew back, full of storm, and a cloud passed over her face. Peering toward the temple, she quivered with dread.

"The god hears, and is angry!" she whispered. With this she turned away, fleeing down the steps of the city gate, toward the shelter of Tebit's house.

CHAPTER
EIGHT

Since his father's death, Mahlon had been the head of
Naomi's household. He, therefore, had no one to
please, in the choice of a wife, but conscience and
the will of Jehovah.

The night Ruth had turned from him, he had
become more determined than ever to make her his
own. Try as he might, there was no forgetting her
touch, or the sound of her voice.

Regarding the will of his God, tradition was no im-
pediment. It was true that Israelite women were not
allowed to marry men of Ammon or Moab. But Israelite men could take the daughters of the desert as
their brides. And as for the matter of Ruth's devotion
to a pagan deity, proselytism was not a requirement
of Jewish law for foreign wives.

Strange, he mused, that for all the warnings concerning women of Moab, neither Moses nor Joshua
had ever set an edict against them. Perhaps they
knew, as he did, that not every Moabitess was shal-
low of spirit. Indeed, he was convinced that though
her culture had marked her with grief, Ruth was a
treasure before the Lord, and would one day shine in
his sight.

One more thing he knew, however. Tebit would be
persuaded to release Ruth only by the smell of

money. And so he set about to win her by earning a small fortune. And when it was accumulated, he would lay it at the weaver's feet, in purchase of his bride.

He passed down her street this evening, guiding his lightly laden donkey more slowly than necessary. In the small bundles on the creature's back were the only wares which he had not sold at market this afternoon. Since the donkey had carried four times the load on her way to the square that morning, it was clear that Mahlon had experienced a fine day of trade, and the bag upon his belt was swollen with revenue.

He paused as he drew near Ruth's house, hoping to catch a glimpse of her. There was no sign of life in the little shop out front, and he could see no further into the premises which closed about a private court.

His shoulders slumped in disappointment, but just as quickly he straightened them and patted the purse on his waist. She would be his, he assured himself. She could not have forgotten his witness for Jehovah; this retreat into Chemoshism was out of fear alone.

Still he stared sadly at the ground as he continued past her abode, until a soft light from the upper story fell across his path, and he lifted his eyes in a flutter of anticipation.

Yes, it must be her chamber window, he reasoned. Only this opening faced the square, and if he stood still long enough, perhaps he would see her at the casement.

In a moment, his wish was granted, for a shadow passed over the window, and then he could observe

her clearly. The lady studied the night sky, running
an ivory comb through her lustrous locks.

Mahlon had never seen Ruth's hair unfastened,
hanging loose about her shoulders. Always she had
worn it bundled at the back of her neck, smooth
against her head. He had not realized how long and
full her tresses were, and only in this light, with the
luxury of the witness, was he able to appreciate the
fullness of her beauty.

If he had loved her before, he was mad for her now,
and all the energy of his manhood longed to be expressed.

He almost cried out to her, but stifled the impulse,
preferring the secret pleasure of the moment.

Ruth placed her comb upon the sill and leaned a bit
further toward the street. Her face bore a somber aspect, which, while not detracting from her radiance,
stirred Mahlon's sympathies. And once again he
wished to lift her up, to speak peace as he always
had.

Her pale green sleeping tunic was loose about her
form, but distinctly feminine, and the slack at the top
revealed her supple neck, draping down to bare
shoulders touched by the desert moon. As she studied
the city, her dark hair fell across her bosom, and
Mahlon was caught by the effect. He would have
called to her now, except that once more her countenance prevented him, and his soul moved with
compassion.

It was the temple which troubled her. As quickly as
she spied it, her hand reached for the shade, to shut
out the brooding sight. She had told him that at night

the temple peak haunted her if she did not close her shade.

Reflexively, the man moved toward her. "Ruth!" he cried. "Do not go!"

Halting, she peered toward the avenue. "Mahlon?" she called. "Is that you?"

"It is, my lady!" he replied. "Do not turn away!"

Ruth studied him sadly and shook her head. "It is not good between us," she explained. "We are of two different worlds."

Mahlon stepped close to her house and beckoned toward the window. "You will see!" he declared. "My God holds *all* worlds in his hand! Let me take you to myself, and you will see!"

The lady stood unmoving for a moment, and he spoke more forthrightly. "Tomorrow I meet with Tebit," he called. "But not against your will. Say you will have me, Ruth."

The Moabitess faltered, glancing anxiously toward the temple spire. A shadow passed over her face, but she fought it.

Turning to Mahlon, she sighed, and a smile replaced the cloud.

"I could never be an Israelite," she warned.

Mahlon shuffled, his eyes twinkling.

"To be my wife will do for now," he assured her. "Everything in its own time."

PART II
Seedtime

How blessed is the one who does not walk in the
    counsel of the wicked,
Nor stand in the path of sinners,
Nor sit in the seat of scoffers!
But his delight is in the law of the Lord,
And in his law he meditates day and night.

PSALM 1:1, 2
(Author's paraphrase)

CHAPTER ONE

Naomi bent over the old pottery wheel in the rooftop corner and lifted the dusty linen from its spindle. She shook it gingerly over the balustrade and wiped the summer sweat from her brow.

"Two of them!" she muttered. "Elimelech — my heart will not survive it!"

No one intruded upon her solitude, or questioned who it was to whom she spoke. But she was not alone. The specter of her departed husband was always available in this private place. And here she could speak her mind.

"Perhaps, my love, in a thousand years, I could have learned to tolerate *one* of them," she supposed. "But two women of Moab! In this Jewish house! I shall never get past it!"

Her sharp gray eyes had seen enough this afternoon to wither her spirit. Chilion had bought his new bride a festival gown, preparing her for yet another Moabite celebration. And like a streetwalker, Orpah had flashed through the court of Naomi's house, parading her brazen self before the eyes of both brothers. Though Ruth had been present, she had only looked on quietly, and while Naomi could have admired the young woman's patience, she took it as an indication of tolerance for Orpah's lewd behavior.

The day Mahlon announced to his mother his choice of a wife, the old woman's spirit had crumbled. She knew very well that, should her firstborn take a Moabite wife, there would be no stopping Chilion from doing the same. If he had ever feared that Mahlon would stand in his way, he realized now that his elder brother could say little against his decision.

And so, it had all happened quickly. Only a small company of Kir-Hareseth Jews attended the double wedding, and it was a muted occasion, many of the women offering Naomi their condolences rather than congratulations.

Both brides' parents were there, awkward with the ceremony and its implications. Though they were not giving their daughters over to Judaism, they were releasing them to an alien subculture. Indeed, despite the girls' ardent petitioning, the two fathers, who had supported each other's business ventures, never would have allowed the marriages—had the Jewish brothers not already begun to show financial promise. And the elder gentlemen intended to watch after their young ladies' welfare with anxious care.

On the Moabite side, therefore, the wedding was also an event of somberness, rather than gaiety. If Ruth and Orpah sensed their parents' stiffness, however, they were only beginning to know the strain of this cross-cultural bond.

From the moment they stood beneath the canopy, they entered a world awesome in its demands. Though Ruth's heart was well ahead of her background, Naomi could not see it. To her mind Orpah and Ruth were sisters, two of a kind. And she would exact from them strict obedience, treating them less like daughters-in-law than the pagans she judged them to be.

After all, she reasoned, they were Moabite, and Moab was root-rotten. The decendants of an incestuous union between Abraham's nephew, Lot, and his eldest daughter. "Arisen from Sodom, and brothers of Gomorrah," she insisted.

Usually the elderly Jewess waited until evening to go to the rooftop. Today, however, she was stressed beyond all patience. She would seek the solace of times past and cast her gaze toward Judah before the sun set.

Caressing the smooth plate of the potter's wheel, she closed her eyes and turned about, opening them when she felt the Moab sun to her back, and the hot breeze off Zoar to her face.

The Judean hills were visible beyond the summer haze which rippled up in waves from the Dead Sea shore. She knew that Shiloh, holy city of Israel, lay to the north of those hills. But it could have been a full planet away, so remote was her chance of going there.

And then just three days' journey from Shiloh, to the south, was Bethlehem, home of her forefathers.

She smiled, absorbing the memories like a balm, and she raised her eyes to the faraway shepherd fields and sleepy town, seen now only in fantasy. She recalled how her mother had first taken her to the nearby sepulcher of Rachel, favorite wife of the patriarch Jacob. And she remembered the early lessons of approaching womanhood, instilled at her mother's knee.

"Be kind and tenderhearted," the good lady had counseled. "Beauty is deceitful and charm is vain. But the price of a virtuous wife is above rubies."

How true those words had proven to be! Naomi was no beauty, and never had been. But she had captured the eyes of Elimelech, her choice from childhood. And their marriage had been spiced with intimacy, laced with love.

Conveniently, she pushed aside the reality that their last years together had been anything but precious. Whenever that fact pricked her conscience, she lay it at Elimelech's feet. After all, should he have expected the softness of rose petals, and not the sting of thorns? He had uprooted and transplanted Naomi's full-blossomed love from the fertile land west of Jordan to these dry Moab sands. And here she had withered — her fragrance dissipated, her color gone.

She could not be blamed if her husband had begun to wither beside her. She could not be held responsible for shrinking from his caress, or for turning from his kiss.

She had been a good wife. But there were those who would never be such. Especially as she considered Chilion's new bride, her spirit curdled. "She will do him evil and not good, all the days of his life!" she murmured, her face wrinkling in a scowl.

Suddenly, her body moved into an arc, bent under the weight of urgency, and her fingers touched her forehead. She bowed several times toward Shiloh, and shuddered with dread. "Thou art holy, and thy name is holy!" she intoned a rapid prayer. "And the holy ones praise thee every day. Selah! Blessed are thou, Jehovah God, Holy One!" she chanted in minor chords.

Over and over her back bent with the rhythmic song, as though assisting her to say with those words what she could say with no other.

Tears spilled over her aged cheeks, and she did not perceive the soft footfalls on the staircase leading to her housetop sanctuary.

Quietly her other daughter-in-law, the weaver's child, approached from the second story. She had been looking for Naomi, to ask what she needed from market. Having searched the house over, Ruth had determined that the roof was the only place she might be.

But she had not meant to intrude upon the woman's prayers.

She would have turned to leave, happy to avoid some abrasive rebuke, had she not been struck by the phrases which filled the meditation.

"God of our fathers, our King and the King of our fathers," Naomi sang, the music now less melancholy. "Our Creator, our help and our deliverer. . . . Thy name is from everlasting, and there is no God beside thee."

Slowly, with this traditional psalm, the woman straightened her back until her face was filled with departing sunlight, and her hands were raised toward heaven.

Her wrinkled visage glistened still with tears, but the heaviness of her countenance had been lifted, and as she stooped over the potter's wheel again, covering it with the cloth, she sighed with a sense of deliverance.

Ruth

Ruth stood in the stairwell, barely peering over the housetop, and marveled at the transformation. But as Naomi moved to leave the roof, the girl disappeared without a word.

CHAPTER
TWO

Naomi succeeded admirably in her attempts to make
life difficult for Ruth and Orpah. It would not have
been easy for any Gentile bride to perform up to code
in a Jewish household. But the matron appeared to be
bent on making it impossible to please her.

It seemed every act of daily routine must be
managed by a formula, from the way one faced when
rising in the morning (always to the west) to the way
one washed one's hands (always under pouring water
and not in water left standing in a basin). And then
there were the endless injunctions regarding the
family's religious rituals, mandatory tithes, the scrupulous, yet seemingly hypocritical rules regarding
environmental cleanliness, and so on.

The Moabite women found it hard to understand,
for instance, why it mattered so, whether incense was
burned before or after prayers. They were curious as
to why one-tenth of everything, from their husbands'
endowments for household expenses, to the little bags
of anise and mint, must be divided out and set aside
for the Rabbi. What the old gentleman, the austere
leader of the local Jewish assembly, did with the
tithed herbs and spices, they did not know. But they
certainly were not allowed to question. And then, the
brides, already burdened by household drudgery,

were further encumbered with pointless rites of purification.

Ruth chafed under the obligation of weekly washing the *outsides* of vessels and cups. Indeed, it often seemed more important to perform this act than to cleanse the insides of the containers after using them at mealtime.

But the weaver's daughter had determined that neither such inconveniences nor Naomi's ill humor would completely alienate her. Whether it was due more to Mahlon's consistent, loving witness, or the surges of her own hungry heart, she could not tell. But she had been indelibly impressed by the words of Naomi's prayer the day she came upon her rooftop meditation. And she must know more about the Jewish faith.

If the matron noticed the sudden proximity of Ruth, standing at her elbow, offering help with her work time and again, ready to fetch and carry, it was several days into the phenomenon before she commented.

At first she spurned the attention, greeting every friendly act with suspicion, every bit of aid with condescension. Since Orpah was much less apt to be at hand than Ruth, however, their hours together were rarely interrupted; and as it became clear that the girl would not be put off easily, the old woman was obliged to accept her nearness with less reluctance.

Ruth's attempts at conversation began as idle chitchat, observations on the weather, unusual interest in the matron's kosher recipes, repeated requests for instructions regarding this household task or that.

The first time the bride worked up courage to approach a deeper topic, it was evidence of just how much she longed for knowledge. For to this point Naomi had still received her overtures coldly, giving her no reason to expect openness.

However, the day the opportunity for boldness presented itself, the Moabitess took it eagerly.

The sons of Elimelech had been commissioned by the palace of Kir-Hareseth to enter their wares in a competition. It seemed the king desired a set of urns for his winery, and wished to select his potter based on the best examples of such work in the city. Though Mahlon and Chilion had only begun to establish a reputation independent of their father's, they were quickly becoming known for their products, and were among the few who would be given the chance to bid.

"Hmph!" Naomi snorted when Mahlon gave the news at breakfast. "Your father's art in the house of Chemosh!"

And with this she left the table, shuffling angrily toward the kitchen.

"Not our *father's* work!" Mahlon cried after her. "This is to be the work of my hands and Chilion's!"

"All the same!" Naomi rebutted, drawing the archway curtain closed behind her.

Mahlon, who reclined at the meal, slumped back into his low couch with a sigh. And Ruth stroked his brow with a cool hand.

"She will never understand that we do not live in Judah!" he complained, shaking his head. "Nor did we bring Israel with us in our satchels!"

Ruth smiled quietly and nodded toward the arch. "She is lonely," she offered. "Be patient with her."

But at this, Orpah bristled. "How can you defend her?" she spat, dabbing her lips with a napkin and tossing it onto the table. "The woman has treated us like lepers since the day we came here. If she is lonely, it is because she makes everyone miserable. I, for one, have no sympathy!"

Mahlon started, offended at Orpah's tone, and Chilion leaned forward protectively.

"Enough!" Ruth pleaded. "Let's say no more."

By afternoon, everyone had departed, the two brothers for their work, and Orpah to dawdle at the bazaar.

Ruth sat with her mother-in-law over a bundle of mending, running a needle through one of Mahlon's tunics. She held it fondly, reveling in the knowledge that she was the owner's wife.

Naomi was typically distant, caught up in her own troubles, and she sighed absently as she worked a thread through one of Chilion's garments.

"At least you mend your own husband's clothes," the old woman grumbled. "Orpah should be doing this!"

Ruth ignored her tone, glad that for once the matron could say something in her favor.

"I am happy to serve Mahlon," she replied. "He is a wonderful man."

On this they could agree, and Naomi drew her shoulders back proudly. "Indeed," she admitted.

"With a fine future," Ruth added.

"True," the mother concurred.

"But you do not wish for him to apply to the king's commission?"

A sudden silence, more substantial than the distance between them, hung in the air. Naomi glanced sharply at the girl.

"You have understood correctly."

Ruth fidgeted with her needle, working it at an awkward angle. "Is it true," she managed, "that there is no king in Israel? And never has been?"

The mother-in-law did not know how to interpret the question. Jews were scorned throughout Palestine for their peculiar governmental system. Indeed, they had never been a kingdom, and were a rarity in the world.

Yet, the girl seemed to bear no malice in her tone, and Naomi thought carefully before responding.

"We are a peculiar treasure unto Jehovah," she explained, not caring how her daughter-in-law would take the designation. "Our God sends us leaders for each generation, and they speak for him to us."

Ruth contemplated the notion with a knitted brow. "But, does not every culture have such leaders? Why, the priests of Chemosh interpret his will daily in Moab's court."

Naomi flinched at the comparison, but for once bridled her animosity.

"Israel has a tribe of priests, called Levites, who perform the services of worship and atonement," she answered. "But only our judges and our prophets interpret for the Lord of all the earth."

"Ah, yes, 'judges.' They are not the same as kings?"

"No, indeed," Naomi objected. "Jehovah is our King! But," she said, lowering her eyes and speaking more softly, "he knows our frailties, and that it is difficult for mere mortals to grasp the notion of an in-

visible monarch. So," she sighed and looked heavenward, "he has appointed these officers to preside over
the affairs of Israel. Judges, they are called, but not
mere dispensers of justice. Tribal leaders handle our
legal cases, but our judges are the very agents of
divine will on *all matters*."

Ruth listened respectfully. "Perhaps they are like
the *shufetim* of Phoenicia. I have heard that they
serve beneath the king. . . ."

"No!" Naomi corrected, interrupting the analogy.
"There is no real comparison. You see," she reiter-
ated, "Jehovah is our King, not some man, and the
judges are dependent on him. In this lies the secret of
their strength!"

It was no use. Ruth could not fathom the concept.
To her a god was a god, a king a king, and anything
less must be a vassal. That a nation's deity should
also be its monarch was inconceivable.

"Mother," she addressed her with the common
term, "I . . . I came upon you yesterday, when you
were at your prayers."

Naomi studied her narrowly and Ruth was quick to
add, "Oh, I had not intended to do so. And I would
have turned to leave immediately, except that I was
caught by your words, and found myself listening
closely."

The old woman, while still doubtful of the girl's
motives, was surprised at her interest. "Yes, what did
you hear?" she asked.

"Words similar to what you speak today. That your
God is your King, and the King of your fathers. That
he is from everlasting, and . . . that there is no God
beside him." Ruth's heart caught in her throat as she

recited the phrases. "I surely do not do justice to your song of prayer. I can only remember parts of it."

Naomi was stunned that any Moabitess would be intrigued by such a thing and that, on once hearing such words, they could have penetrated her mind.

"Yes," she whispered, "it is a traditional psalm. I learned it from my father and my mother, and the elders in Bethlehem. Sometimes," she acknowledged, "it is easy for a hymn to become mere formality, especially when one has heard it all one's life. But, this prayer . . . it always moves me."

Ruth nodded, an excited gleam in her eye. "Oh, Mother, I could see that yesterday! Why, it was like a miracle, the change in your countenance. . . ."

As soon as she had said this, she drew back, fearful that she had become too intimate in her observations.

And Naomi would have taken offense. But it was difficult, as she began to know the young woman, to bear malice toward her. Strange as it seemed, it appeared the Moabitess had feelings deeper than any pagan should.

The mother-in-law made no retort, only turning to her mending, and Ruth quietly sighed relief.

Dare she ask another question? Perhaps, if she kept the widow speaking on politics, she could glean something more from her.

"These judges," she risked, "they are chosen by the people?"

Naomi set down her needle, and looked wide-eyed at the girl. "You are truly interested in my nation?" she asked. "But, why?"

Ruth shrugged, her face burning. "Because . . .

because I married an Israelite," she stammered. "It is my duty to learn all I can about his people—so . . . so that I might be a satisfactory wife."

Naomi noted the uneasiness with which the girl framed her alibi. But she could not imagine Ruth's true motivation.

Shaking her head, she simply replied, "The judges can be chosen by popular election, as in the case of Jephthah. Some are named to the office by a prophet. Some simply declare themselves, perhaps proving their worthiness in war. But in each case, we know that the Lord has raised them up."

Ruth thought on this statement a moment. "Raised them up?" she marveled.

"Indeed," the matron explained. "We are a stiffnecked people, prone to sin despite God's blessing. Often we have been sold into the hands of our enemies. But when we cry out, Jehovah raises up a deliverer, and we have rest."

The old woman's eyes traveled toward the street wall, and Ruth sensed her descending sorrow. For the first time, she could grasp what it must be like for the elderly Jewess, trapped in an alien land. And now she knew the meaning of her prayers.

A deliverer? Ruth could not conceive of petitioning for such a thing. Chemosh did not deal in deliverers or in rest.

Chemosh was not like Naomi's God.

CHAPTER
THREE

Ruth labored over the peculiar dough of the matzoh bread, patting it repeatedly into a stiff, unrising cake. She observed Naomi's adept fingers as they worked the tacky substance, and she wondered why everything must be done with such care.

Passover would be upon them in a few hours, and since before dawn the three women of Mahlon's household had been in the midst of preparations. Whole roasted lamb, even to the intestines, a salad of bitter herbs, and unleavened bread were the staples. But through the years other very eccentric items had been added to the menu, and must be prepared with specific care. Charoseth sauce—a mixture of vinegar, figs, almonds, dates, raisins, and spice—beaten to the consistency of mortar, commemorated the toils of the Hebrews in the Egyptian brickyards. And, indeed, every bit of fare bore some symbolic significance, which one must be raised in the culture to appreciate.

Orpah was impatient with the whole procedure. She sighed as she followed Naomi's scrupulous instructions, and occasionally it appeared she might actually leave the work to her mother-in-law, so often did she stop, hands on hips, glaring contemptuously at the old matron.

"I simply do not understand all this!" she objected. "When the children of Chemosh have a celebration,

they merely enjoy themselves. Why all this finicki-
ness?"

Ruth could sense Naomi's rising temperature.
While she had similar questions, she kept them to
herself, realizing how seriously the elder took the
whole affair.

"I shall not waste my breath with another explanation!" Naomi snapped. "You do not really care to
learn our ways. Just do as I say, and tomorrow you
will be free to roam the street with the other harlots."

Ruth cringed and braced herself for the reper-
cussion.

It came with a shriek, Orpah's long neck red with
anger, and her eyes flaming.

"It must be easy for you to call me such things!"
she cried. "You, who have not set foot outside this
house for years! Any girl who experiences life would
seem a harlot to a dead woman!"

Naomi steadied herself, and then stepped back,
lifting her ladle in a tight fist. "Hussy!" she bellowed.
"You will be the end of Chilion and all who dwell
here! Out of my kitchen!"

Orpah flashed blazing eyes. "Gladly!" she declared,
tossing her apron on the floor and flying through the
arch toward the court.

Chilion met her there, perplexed and indignant.
And as Mahlon came upon them, he was surprised to
hear his brother rebuke the Moabitess.

"You will apologize!" he was demanding, pointing
her back toward the cooking room. "Can you not
hold your tongue for one day? At least honor our
Passover, if nothing else!"

But Orpah would not be corrected. Pushing past her husband, she raced up the gallery stairs.

"Madness!" she called over her shoulder. "This house is mad! I will not waste my youth on bitter herbs and matzoh balls! I have better things to do than worry over how much cumin to put to how much anise, or whether a lamb is blemished or not. Who cares for such things?" she raved. "When the hide is off, I can't tell a lamb from a nursling hog!"

Chilion stood helpless on the patio, numb with the consequence of past choice. Mahlon had no word of comfort, and even if he had, could not have given it, for just then, Naomi came rushing from the kitchen.

"Blasphemy!" she screamed. "Mahlon, do something! Did you hear the whore?"

The elder brother only nodded mutely as Naomi squalled, her fingers tearing at her gray hair. "She compared our lamb to a pig, Mahlon! Our holy sacrifice to an unclean animal!"

"I heard, Mother," he assured her. "Let it be."

"Let it be?" she cried. "She has blasphemed your father's house, and all the laws of Moses!"

Mahlon sighed and turned angrily to Chilion, looking for a way to relieve himself. "Can you not control your wife?" he snarled.

Chilion could have made a retort, but instead hung his head in shame.

Naomi was still seething with anger as Mahlon escorted her back to the kitchen. "Clear your mind of this, now," he insisted. "She is only a Moabitess, after all. She could not know better."

But just as he spoke these words, parting the arch

curtain, he was caught by Ruth's wounded expression.

"I . . . I didn't mean . . . , " he stammered.

The girl only turned to her work, her shoulders a little stooped. And Mahlon cursed himself.

CHAPTER
FOUR

Ruth sat on the low pallet which had been her bridal
bed, grooming her hair with a fine-bristled brush.

The strokes she made with it were more firm and
rapid than usual, her face clouded with resentment.

She had looked forward to the evening's celebration
with eagerness, hoping that it would shed more light
on Mahlon's religion. But the entire affair had been a
disappointment, tinged as it was by the strain between herself and her husband. She had been unable
to appreciate the nuances of meaning behind the reci-
tations introducing each part of the meal and each
round of drinks.

It was apparent that Mahlon wished to make up to
her for his rash remark at the kitchen door. Frequently, during the feast, he had looked her way and
reached out to touch her. But Ruth had kept to herself, letting the traditional structure of the evening
occupy her.

As host of the table, Mahlon had been responsible
for carrying out the customs of the celebration. Upon
pouring a cup of wine for everyone, he had proceeded, with his mantle drawn over his head, to pro-
nounce a blessing. Then, taking a small swatch of
bitter herbs, he dipped it in the sauce and gave thanks
for the fruits of the earth. Dinner thus commenced,
Mahlon gave the traditional explanation of the feast

and led in a hymn of praise. Thereafter, throughout the meal, he pronounced further blessings, led more singing, and followed each cup of wine with yet another prayer.

Ruth's heart had been stirred by his mellow, confident voice, and the basic history lesson reconstructed by his monologues had not been wasted on her.

But the spirit of the holiday was lost, and it became a perfunctory affair for all involved.

Sad that it should be so, she mused, drawing the brush one final time through her lustrous locks. The moon was bright over Moab, being a season of celebration in this country and throughout the Jordan region. Spring was a stage of new life and anticipation. In a few days, the temple square of Chemosh would ring once more with riot and frivolity.

Ruth was torn by loyalty to her nation and a sense of relief that, if she chose, she could bow gracefully out of participation in its rites. As the wife of a Jew, she was not obliged to maintain her old attachments.

But she knew her parents would seek for her at the coming festival. And Orpah would surely give her a hard time if she opted to stay home.

Ruth placed the brush aside and thought on the poor girl who was now her sister-in-law.

She would never forget Orpah's awkwardness at the Passover meal. Chilion had apparently reprimanded her severely and had insisted she attend the family feast, like it or not. And she was obliged to come dressed appropriately.

It was customary that participants in the paschal supper be garbed as for a journey, in traveling cloaks

and with shoes upon their feet. This was to com-
memorate the original Passover, when the children of
Israel prepared for their flight from Egypt.

How odd it all seemed to the Moabite wives, especially to Orpah, who was accustomed to donning the
flimsiest of party gowns, and the very lightest
sandals, which were to be unloosed and laid aside at
mealtime.

Nor was she allowed to recline upon her dinner
couch, but must, by custom, sit erect like the others,
in memory of the readiness of Moses' people that
long ago night.

Indeed, even Ruth saw little to commend the affair
as a "celebration." What she did glean from the
proceedings was merely another reference to Israel's
national theme. For the Passover story was the most
poignant tale of deliverance and salvation told among
the Hebrews, and reinforced from generation to
generation the notion that they were Jehovah's
"Chosen Race," his "peculiar treasure."

Tonight Ruth battled conflicting needs. Except for
her most painful memory, the loss of little Pekah, life
in Moab had been good to her.

And Moab was synonymous with Chemosh.

This deity and another, Baal Peor, his nearest kin
in the Transjordan pantheon, were very ancient gods,
rooted in the legendary cities of Sodom and Gor-
morrah.

Ruth stood up and stepped to the window of Mahlon's chamber. He would be arriving soon for bed,
and despite her anger, her heart stirred at the anticipation of his touch.

She looked over the rooftops toward Kir-Hareseth's

southwestern wall. Beyond that boundary, across miles of desert skirting the Dead Sea's eastern rim, were flat plains where the ancient cities of Zoar once stood. Sodom was no more, and Gomorrah had vanished with her. No one knew just how they had been destroyed. There were no remnants, not even a hint of rubble. But everyone in Palestine, Egypt, and Syria knew they had once existed.

Moab had her roots in that world, the world of Abraham. A hybrid race they were, the offspring of Lot's relation with his eldest daughter, a virgin of Sodom.

A blush rose to Ruth's face. She had been taught to take pride in her ancestry, that the origins of Moab were holy. After all, did not its royal house flourish on the liaisons of kings and princesses? The occasional idiot born to the palace, or the deformed infant presented by one of the king's daughters, was only a special treasure to be offered on the altar of Chemosh's fire.

Ruth gripped the window ledge and closed her eyes. *Fire! Always the fire!*

Moab had been born in fire, in the ashes of Sodom and the smoke of Gomorrah.

Moab, son of Lot, had been born in the heat of lust and incestuous passion.

To this day, his memory was exalted in the flames of altar pyres and the sulphur of sacrifice.

Suddenly, Ruth longed for Mahlon's voice and for the kindness of his eyes. Turning, she found him in the doorway, and her heart raced.

He was in silhouette, framed by the hall light spilling past him. He still wore his mantle over his head, as he had done at dinner when reading from the Scriptures. And he seemed now the most holy of men.

Ruth trembled as he approached and hesitated as he reached for her.

But Mahlon drew her tenderly to himself, and bending down, pressed her cheek to his.

"Tears, my lady?" he whispered. "Have I been so cruel?"

"Oh, my lord," Ruth said with a sigh, raising her gaze to his moon-glinted eyes, "you only spoke the truth. I am but a Moabitess, and cannot please you so well as one of your own race." Mahlon shook his head, but she continued. "Indeed, I am not worthy of you, husband."

Withdrawing from his arms, she looked once more toward the south, to the environs of the extinguished cities, a shiver crossing her shoulders.

Mahlon, bewildered, stepped close. "I do not know your mind, my lady, nor the thoughts which sadden you tonight. But I do know your heart. And though there are many fine women in Israel, you far outshine them all."

Ruth bowed her head, a tear falling onto the windowsill. But Mahlon turned her about and lifted her chin with his fingertips. Bending close, he breathed gently upon her neck, and brought his lips to hers.

CHAPTER FIVE

The King's Highway, connecting Damascus and points east with Transjordan, linked Kir-Hareseth with its neighbor, Ar, to the north. The only other fortified city in Moab, Ar was commercial cousin to the capital and had a good market for Mahlon's wares.

Today he had leased a space at that town's bazaar, and was eager to set up before noon.

Ruth rode beside him on the seat of his heavily laden wagon. She had never accompanied him outside Kir-Hareseth. Chilion usually went with him to distant places, but was staying home to complete the collection the brothers would enter in royal competition.

The morning sun cast a wide shadow west from the wagon, which traversed the "field of Moab." This naturally enclosed plateau, bordered by the Arnon, the Jordan, and a small ring of southeastern hills, was most lovely in spring. During winter it was bleak; and in summer, much too hot for comfort. But this season it made wonderful pastureland. As the couple crossed it, the pinks of morning were just giving way to the brilliant green which robed its hills and dales.

Small pillows of white scattered here and there moved, heads down, nibbling at moist blades of grass, and only when a black face was raised among them, or a small skittering lamb frolicked out from the group, were they identifiable as sheep.

Mahlon watched them wistfully. "Your king is a sheep-breeder, is he not?" he asked.

"Yes," Ruth nodded, noting that even though her husband had lived most of his life in Moab, he would never consider its monarch his own. "The tradition goes far back in our history. We did, after all, begin as a shepherd race, and our towns are quite new."

"Indeed," the Jew recalled. "In Israel some interpret 'Kir-Hareseth' as 'new city,' rather than 'city of pottery.'"

Ruth smiled. "It can mean either, I suppose, depending on where one places the accent. Perhaps it was a play on words from the beginning."

Mahlon agreed, and then grew contemplative. "You know," he said, "I imagine that when foreigners chance upon our two nations, they find much more in common between us than not."

Ruth studied him in surprise. "How so, my lord?"

"We, like you, are largely a shepherd race," he began. "One of my strongest memories of my hometown is the rolling hills which frame it and the many sheep which graze there." His eyes took on a faraway aspect. "In fact, as a child I dreamed of being a herdsman."

Ruth was not surprised, knowing her husband to be a quiet and solitary man.

But he continued, "And our languages are so similar as to be almost twins."

Ruth nodded, not daring to mention the vast disparities between their laws, their government, and their sense of tradition, to say nothing of their religions. Meanwhile, Mahlon's face bore an expression of reverence and almost of zeal.

"But more important than any of this," he declared, "we are related to Abraham!"

Ruth observed, "We are only distant cousins, are we not? Our patriarch Lot was only Abraham's nephew, while your Isaac was his son."

"True," Mahlon assented. "But he loved Lot as his own. Likely it was across this very field that Abraham pursued the four kings of the east to rescue Lot from slavery."

The story was familiar to Israelite and Moabite alike. The tale of the Mesopotamian confederacy which had swept through Transjordan, subjugating its people, was an ancient one. And the forefather of Moab, Abraham's nephew, had been one of its captives until his uncle, with only a handful of soldiers, defeated them and chased them to the north of Damascus.

"I am pleased that you see things as you do," Ruth said softly. "There are not many Jews who would consider Moabites their brethren. But, husband, there are such antagonisms between our people."

"As there often are between brothers," he acknowledged. "It seems that those who are closest usually see little but their own differences."

Ruth perceived the sadness behind his comment.

"You think of Chilion, don't you?" she asked.

"Rivalry between brothers seems to run in my family," he explained. "My father left Bethlehem to avoid a feud brewing between his kinsmen, as much as to flee the famine."

Mahlon had never shared much about his relatives

other than to speak highly of Elimelech. Regarding folk left behind in Judea, Ruth knew nothing, and as he described the civil war between his two uncles, she listened respectfully.

It seemed that the two men, Elimelech's elder brothers, had both been wealthy grainfield owners before the famine had hit. The younger of the two had been a better manager than the firstborn, and had not been so hard-pressed financially by the drought. When the eldest had gone bankrupt, he had been forced to turn to the middle son for employment. And though the younger brother had been kind and gracious to the needy man, redeeming his property so that it would remain in the family, and then placing him as its manager, the elder bore him great resentment.

Elimelech, whose personal fortunes were jeopardized by the famine, and who was increasingly uncomfortable with the ongoing feud, had seen flight from Judea as a reasonable solution.

Over the years immediately following his emigration, word from Bethlehem had been replete with references to the escalating battle. Eventually, to everyone's surprise and Elimelech's further distress, the younger brother passed away, and news from home tapered off. What Mahlon's father did hear, indicated that the elder brother had moved his family to a town in a northern province.

His sons, who had been Mahlon and Chilion's childhood enemies, had grown up shiftless ne'er-do-wells, by all accounts. It was reported they still leeched off the generosity of the deceased's solitary heir, a man somewhat older than themselves, who managed his father's business with finesse.

When Mahlon had given Ruth this account, she sighed, feeling his helpless frustration.

"Well," she replied, "if Moab and Israel are kin, they have conducted themselves reasonably. At least our countries have never gone to war against each other, not in the three centuries that we have shared a boundary."

Mahlon, absorbed in thoughts of his family, did not resume the original topic of conversation without an awkward pause. "Yes, of course," he reflected at last, "but there is more than one kind of warfare, my lady. May I remind you that there were nearly two decades during which your people oppressed Israel, after we entered Canaan?" But then, quickly shrugging, he reasoned, "However, that was due to the Lord's strenthing Moab for our discipline."

Ruth looked sideways at her teacher, amazed at his logic. She would never get used to the Jews' sense of their own centrality in the scheme of history.

"Husband," she said as respectfully as possible, "when I was a child, I was taught that we had gained control during that period because *Chemosh* had strengthened us, and certainly not for your benefit!"

Mahlon was stunned by the rebuttal, but quickly rallied. "And you, Ruth? Do you believe that?"

The woman watched the road in angry silence. Why must she always be on the defensive simply because she had married an Israelite? "My lord," she replied at last, a tense edge to her tone, "you know that I am torn between your ways and the ways of my countrymen. On the matter of religion, our two peoples are very different indeed."

The husband studied her sadly. And she, perceiving his longing, felt a blush rise to her face.

"Perhaps it is hopeless, then," he said with a sigh, looking across the desert in resigned defeat. "I had always believed that you could one day be turned to Jehovah."

The Moabitess sensed the ache of his heart and quickly offered, "Oh, Mahlon! I only wish to understand your teachings. I know the ways of Chemosh and they leave my heart cold as stone. I long to trust in your God, but his ways are strange to me."

Suddenly the Israelite's gaze was caught by a distant shrine, one of the many such "high places" scattered about the hills of Moab. And a radiance lit his countenance.

"Look!" he pointed, directing Ruth to observe the stone canopy which sheltered it.

The woman could not imagine what interest he found in the little grotto carved into the desert slope.

"It is only a monument to one of Chemosh's companions," she said. "Probably Baal-Peor."

"Exactly!" Mahlon agreed. "I recall the story my father told of Moses' burial place. It is along a valley in your country, you know. Near one of these very shrines, a house of Baal-Peor! Don't you see?"

Ruth shook her head, failing to derive any great meaning from the legend. "Yes, I have heard that your lawgiver died before reaching Canaan, in the land of Moab."

Mahlon stopped the wagon and drew his donkey to the roadside, the heavy earthen vessels clanking in their burlap wrappers. Facing toward the little altar-place, he exclaimed, "It was from such a height and near such a sanctuary that Moses caught his only glimpse of the Holy Land!"

Then, directing Ruth to study the western horizon, he declared. "It matters not where you were born, or how you were raised, my lady. Even if you stand in Chemosh's shadow, Jehovah is not out of reach. So long as you can see Israel, the one true God is not far away!"

CHAPTER
SIX

The land! Always the land! Ruth thought. Perhaps, after all, she could never be a proper Jewess since she had never lived in Israel.

This evening she tended the fire in Naomi's court, hoping to ward off an unseasonably chilly wind which blew down from the housetop. Ever since their return from Ar, where Mahlon had sold every one of his wares, the husband had been preoccupied with preparations for the king's contest. And Ruth had been alone with maudlin introspection.

It was no use, she reasoned. Moab and Israel might be cousins, but no Moabite was privy to the oracles of the peculiar nation west of Jordan. Try as she might, she would never understand the Jew's attachment to land and history.

And why should she care, after all? Was not Moab the stronger nation? Did not all of the surrounding countries consider Israel weak? The region of the Jews was a divided land, notorious for internal squabbles and tribal competition. No single contingency held preeminence. And it often seemed that civil discord could lose the Israelites their territory completely.

Other nations watched them like birds of prey, ready to swoop at the next opportunity. And the ancient Canaanites still held sizable tracts in strategic positions throughout the provinces.

Still Ruth's spirit struggled. Naomi's reluctant tolerance for the young wife did not sway her in favor of Judaism, yet she could not disregard the fervid insistence that Yahweh was the only God, King of all the earth, the insistence that he was intimately involved in all matters personal, as well as national.

But what drew her most was Mahlon's love and the emptiness of her own faith, the crushing reality that the way of Chemosh was a joyless way, holding out promise only to the stripping of the soul.

Grabbing a handful of kindling, Ruth snapped it angrily between her fists and cast it into the firepit. Sparks reflected in her green eyes, spreading an orange glow across the mist of tears which welled there. She did not preceive Naomi's presence until the old woman bent close.

"I said, 'Did you have to pay dearly for the firewood today?' " the Jewess repeated.

Ruth, startled into the present, nodded her head. "Being past the season, it cost more than usual," she replied.

The mother-in-law settled on a nearby bench and watched the girl curiously, making a rare personal comment.

"You were always the quiet one," she began, "but ever since you returned from Ar, you have had even less to say."

Ruth gazed into the flames and tried not to tremble. But Naomi was unusually observant tonight and leaned forward, studying the young woman's damp lashes. "Why—you have been crying!" she said softly. "What ails you?"

"I feel fine, Mother," Ruth feigned a smile. "It is only that the smoke smarted my eyes."

Naomi was not convinced, and for once, she did the pursuing. "My dear," she said carefully, "you have been married over a year now. It would be time for you to be with child. . . ."

Ruth drew back, caught off guard by the idea. "Oh, no," she laughed. "I am not pregnant!" And then, considering the old woman's gentle suggestion, added, "It would be easy to conclude that any emotional upset I might experience could be due to such a thing. But, no, I have watched myself carefully and have seen no signs of motherhood as yet."

Naomi could not hide her disappointment. Though she had fought her sons' choice of women, she hoped that one of her daughters-in-law would soon announce a grandchild, and preferred to think Ruth would be the first. Mahlon was the elder, after all, and should produce the next heir of Elimelech's line.

A small corner of her sided with Mahlon's wife for other reasons. But she was not ready to acknowledge the growing fondness she felt toward Ruth.

"What troubles you?" she prodded again. "You have inquired much of me and my ways. I should like to enter your heart a little, as well."

The girl, moved by this confession, turned wonderingly to Naomi.

"Truly, Mother? I am of interest to you?"

The matron's veneer of Jewish scruple should have barred further intimacy. But the fact was that she enjoyed the Moabitess.

"You *are,* my dear. Just as I have been to you."

The daughter-in-law marveled at this alteration,

but gratefully proceeded to speak her mind.

"I am sad because I fear I shall never be what my husband deserves," she began.

"How is that?" Naomi queried.

"Just as you have surely thought, no Gentile could ever be adequate partner to a Jew."

Indeed, the matron *had* thought this. It had been her bread of sorrow since Chilion had first brought Orpah home. But, strangely, as this young lady who had never given offense put the objection into words, the old woman found herself rebelling.

"Why—child. You have blessed us all!"

Again Ruth was astonished, and Naomi looked away, flush-faced.

"I should have told you so, many times," the elder admitted. "I have borne a hard heart—one which does not please my God."

"But. . . ."

"No—let me acknowledge my sin," Naomi insisted. "I have hidden it behind religion far too long. You see . . . ," she whispered, "I love my nation so, that it has blinded me to the good in other people. I have become a jealous woman—jealous for my God, for my land."

"But," Ruth said respectfully, "is not such jealousy a noble thing?"

Naomi smiled. "Not when it stands between mother and daughter," she said, looking deep into Ruth's bewildered eyes. "I can forgive myself only because when I knew you had been crying, the truth in my heart pushed prejudice aside. I have loved you, my dear, more than I dared admit."

Tears welled along the gray lashes, as a great

weight of bitterness broke. And the young girl reached for her.

For a long moment the women embraced, and then Naomi cleared her throat, pulling away and dabbing her eyes with her sleeve.

"Now," she said firmly, "speak of your troubles."

Ruth studied the pavement of Naomi's court and framed her problem carefully. "You just now referred to your love of nation and land. Of this I should like to know more. I feel that I am unworthy, for I have never set foot in Israel and likely never shall. Mahlon talks as though one cannot know Jehovah apart from bearing that country's dust in his very veins!"

The mother-in-law did not reply quickly. She knew quite well that it was the inclination of her brethren, just as it was hers, to consider God's presence as diminished in proportion to one's distance from Israel.

But when confronted with the issue squarely, she felt a blush rise to her cheeks. "It is difficult for us to be casual about the land," Naomi agreed. "It is the warp and woof of our faith, so that it hardly seems distinguishable from Jehovah himself."

Her gray eyes were sad as she conceded, "And we accuse others of idolatry!"

Ruth did not dissuade her from these self-castigations. She only sat in awe of the woman's un-expected humility. Never would she have dreamed this stalwart Jewess capable of the mellow turn her heart had taken.

But the questions still burned to be answered, and she reached out a hesitant hand to retrieve Naomi's focus.

"Mother, tell me, how does Jehovah deal with your people? Is he predictable? Does sacrifice win his favors?"

She wished a comparison to be drawn between Chemosh and the God of Israel. But the teacher could not. "The one true God takes no pleasure in sacrifice. Nor is he a man to be bought by gifts or through the pain of extremity."

Ruth shook her head. "Why, then, if he loves Israel, does the land not prosper? Pardon me, but yours is not the most stable of nations."

Naomi knew the girl did her a kindness. Indeed, Israel was among the least of the earth in its present state.

"Ha!" Naomi laughed. "I see your point. But if my people struggle now, it is a result of their own folly. And if they pass through the fire, it is to be made pure."

Ruth jolted uncomfortably at the reference to fire, and turned rigidly toward the hearth. Her mother-in-law knew nothing of the tragedy which had marked her young life. Nor would she speak of it now.

"Why?" she asked, gazing into the flames. "Why does Jehovah require such purity?"

The old woman leaned close, as if to share a great secret. Drawing Ruth by the shoulders, she whispered, "Because we are to be the nation of Messiah. We must be worthy of the One who shall spring from Isaac's loins."

"Messiah?" Ruth asked.

"Yes. The 'Anointed One'!" Naomi declared. "Through him all nations shall be blessed, as it was promised our Father Abraham!"

Ruth did not understand. Never had she heard of Messiah.

Just another strange oracle of Mahlon's peculiar people! she reasoned.

But the matron's next words struck her profoundly, as she continued with a fervid expression, "It is the dream of every Jewess to be Messiah's mother. And the dream of every Jewish lad that his betrothed will bear Messiah for his line!"

CHAPTER
SEVEN

Ruth stood before a tall bronze mirror in her father's shop, admiring her reflection and the drape of vivid green which her mother pinned about her torso.

"See! Is it not perfect?" Marta exclaimed. "When I saw it among your father's goods, I knew he had made it specially for you."

"But, *how* do you know?" Ruth asked. "Perhaps it is an order for a client."

Her voice betrayed the hope, however, that this was indeed a fabric meant for her. She could imagine it in a fluid gown, and could imagine Mahlon's face when he saw her wearing it.

"Child, your father speaks of you too often. He misses you so." A warm mist clouded the woman's eyes as she told her daughter this, and as she reached for her embrace.

"And I have missed you both!" Ruth declared, holding her tight. "Life is very difficult in my new home."

Turning to the mirror again, she gathered the fabric to her cheek and sighed. "They speak of strange things, Mother. Things I do not understand."

Marta registered no surprise. "The Jews are an odd race," she acknowledged. "Tebit allowed your marriage only after much consideration."

Ruth smiled, appreciating Marta's respect for her father, but knowing that Mahlon's potential as a moneymaker had played a major part in the man's decision.

"Yes, Mother, I know. But Mahlon will not disappoint you, I am certain. This week he and his brother will be displaying their wares at the palace."

"Truly?" Marta marveled. "They are entering the competition?"

"Indeed. That is all they have thought of for weeks. All their time has been spent on preparations."

Marta smoothed the silk over her daughter's shoulders with an eager hand. "Then, it is well I summoned you today," she said. "We must design a garment for the celebration! What better use to make of this piece?"

"Celebration?" Ruth asked.

"Certainly! You will want to be ready to appear at court when Mahlon's goods are selected by the king."

"Court? Mother, I think you dream."

"No, indeed. I have heard that Mahlon's wares are in great demand. As you say, he will not disappoint us!"

Ruth was grateful for her mother's enthusiasm. It somewhat mollified the sadness that had hung over her in recent days.

"We must hurry!" Marta exclaimed. "Tebit is gone for the morning. Perhaps we can have this done by noon!"

Ruth smiled at the emerald of her own eyes, watching the movement of her mother's hands as the drape was pinned here and tucked there.

She might never give Mahlon a Messiah-son, but she would surely please him with her beauty when she could.

"Mother," she asked hesitantly, "do you ever question your husband's ways?"

Marta glanced up with a peculiar fidget. "Of course not, child. Why do you ask?"

"Because, I question Mahlon's."

"Well," the woman sighed, "I should think so! After all, you are a daughter of Chemosh."

Ruth was glad that her mother was too occupied to notice the crimson flush of her cheeks. But she took a deep breath and confessed, "I question Chemosh as well."

Tebit's wife, working now on the garment's hem, pretended not to hear. "I said, 'I question Chemosh as well,' " Ruth repeated.

Marta trembled, dropping a pin to the floor and then fumbling for it.

"Such a thing is unholy!" she whispered. "Never let your father hear this."

"But, Mother," Ruth demanded, lifting her to her feet, "surely you have had your times of doubt. Especially when Pekah. . . ."

"Enough!" the woman commanded. "We will not speak of this!"

The daughter reluctantly obeyed, turning away and watching Marta's drawn expression in the mirror.

Quickly the seamstress finished the gown, as a tense silence ensued.

"Tell Father," Ruth sighed, changing the subject, "that Mahlon will not disappoint him."

CHAPTER
EIGHT

A few days later, Ruth studied another reflection in another sort of mirror.

Mahlon's handsome face shone back at her in the glaze of a dozen red and amber vessels—small urns, cups, and bowls—as he bent over the display meant for the Chemoshite king.

Children were not such a treasure in Moab as they were in Israel. But just now, Ruth longed with all her being to recreate Mahlon's vitality—to conceive for him a son, a child of comeliness like her husband.

As she stood beside him, she half-consciously pressed the inside of her wrist against her stomach—as though feeling for the life she hoped to harbor there.

Not once since their first wedding anniversary had Mahlon voiced complaint. But surely, in a culture when despite a man's health history, barrenness was solely the woman's burden, he could not help but wonder from time to time why Ruth had not yet blessed him.

"The first year is the year for love," the proverb allowed. "The second for children's sake."

So did many Jews perceive the marriage act. And every man desired his "quiver full" of sons and daughters.

Ruth was determined to accommodate Mahlon in

this way. She hoped that within the weeks following the king's commission, she would be announcing a blessed event.

But today she looked forward to the hour when Mahlon would stand before the king.

The rich glazes and patinas of the little vessels, which her husband had polished for one last time, seemed to promise great things. Mahlon turned to his wife with a smile. Handing her one of his favorite pieces, he bent over her, kissing her tenderly on the cheek.

"Help me load these in the cart," he instructed, directing her to the little vehicle which waited outside the street door.

She could sense his eager excitement as he nestled the gleaming containers into the burlap pillows on the wagon floor.

Orpah stood with Ruth now, as did Chilion. "Go call Mother," the younger brother told his wife, and the haughty Moabitess turned reluctantly to obey.

But Naomi was already on the threshold.

No one need ask the elder woman's thoughts. It was obvious she still did not approve of their catering to a Chemoshite monarch, though she tried to bear a pleasant face.

Fervently Orpah kissed Chilion as he mounted the wagon seat, visions of great wealth flashing through her mind.

And Ruth clung to Mahlon happily. His fine beard was warm to her cheek as he pressed his head to hers.

"Peace," was all he said, and his confident embrace insured success.

CHAPTER
NINE

Ruth never wore her emerald gown for Mahlon, and never stood with him before the king of Moab.

It would never be known whether the sons of Elimelech might have won the commission. For on their way to the palace gate, along the narrow bridge which spanned the lava-strewn moat of Chemosh, all their dreams were dashed.

A peculiar thing it was, an "omen" Naomi would quickly judge, this unforeseen collision, the skidding of wagon wheels, and the crash of cart against nobleman's chariot, as Mahlon's little vehicle crossed the elevated road traversing the Chemoshite chasm.

Quick as that, the lives of the two young Jewish husbands were snuffed out, as their donkey lost his footing and the cart was overturned, falling unceremoniously toward the rocks below.

Of course the nobleman—the "murderer," as Naomi called him—was unscathed, his reputation, like his body, left intact. There was no recourse against his reckless driving in the Moabite courts—surely not for a Jewish widow and her daughters-in-law.

And so, the emerald gown was set aside and the only color to wear was black.

Ruth went through the subsequent hours in a daze. From the moment word was brought of her husband's death, she entered a bewildering fog of grief only intensified by the traditions she was expected to keep, and by the parade of Jewish neighbors who brought unbidden critiques of the incident.

Their analysis of the cause of the untimely deaths need not have been voiced. It was evident in the haughtiness which they camouflaged with a thin veneer of sympathy. But their conclusions were whispered loudly enough, nonetheless.

Of course Jehovah did not approve the brothers' consorting with Moab, they agreed. Mahlon and Chilion had not only married foreign wives, but had then complied with the king's commission, straining the grace of God.

Did not tradition teach that the death of the young is a punishment? they reasoned. Indeed, to succumb before reaching fifty years of age was to be "cut off," like the falling of unripe fruit, or the extinction of a candle. And to meet a sudden death was to be "swallowed up."

Furthermore, to depart without having had a son was to *die,* while to leave behind progeny was merely to "fall asleep."

On all counts, then, it appeared by folk tradition that Mahlon and Chilion had received their just desserts, not having passed away as the righteous should pass, but by the hand of retribution—unlike the death of the sanctified who are "gathered to their fathers."

Such thoughts were not spoken in Naomi's presence. For she was a good woman, by everyone's estimation. And despite the fact that tradition also taught that children suffered according to their parents' sins, no one could presume to accuse either Naomi or Elimelech of transgression.

No—the two brothers had borne their own iniquities and poor Naomi had unjustly suffered more than any transplanted Hebrew should have to endure.

As for the young widows, being daughters of Moab, they deserved only the most cursory condolences. And beyond the traditional rending of the garments, which was Moabite as well as Israelite custom, Ruth and Orpah were lost in a maze of strange procedures as they sought to lay their Jewish husbands to rest.

Because the bodies had been badly abused by the fall from the bridge, they were not kept long in Naomi's house, but were anointed and wrapped for burial as quickly as possible.

All this Ruth helped to perform with her heart in her throat, and in a pall of numbness. She tried not to study Mahlon's broken form too closely, and to avoid looking at the lids which covered his lifeless eyes.

But when they told her that he would be entombed outside the town wall in the sepulcher of the Jews, the shield about her wounded heart began to crack.

The dead of Moab were interred within chambers which were part of each family residence. They were remembered fondly whenever the sealed door was passed. And their bones were sacred, propped against the walls of the domestic tomb in a sitting position, suggestive of rest and readiness.

The dead of Israel were concealed in cold granite, within the maw of the earth. There were no possessions buried to accompany them to the afterlife. And at this neglect, Ruth rebelled.

But, Naomi insisted, all things belong to the righteous and they need take nothing with them from this world. As for the body, it would decay, and served no purpose but to defile. Therefore it must be removed from among the living.

As a child, Ruth had watched the funeral processions of Kir-Hareseth Jews. She had seen how the body was borne upon a bier, far up from the touch of living hands. And she had seen how all Jews along the way, acquaintances or not, joined the parade.

Never had she dreamed that one day she would be among the females to lead such a group.

"Women are at the head of the procession," Naomi explained, as she walked with her black-robed daughters-in-law, "because a woman brought death into the world."

Orpah looked straight ahead as the elder said this, her face ashen against her ebony mantle, and against the frame of coal-dark hair which peeked from beneath. Ruth studied her Moabite sister and wondered what she thought.

As for herself, she would have questioned Jewish reasoning on this point, had the time been more opportune. *Had woman not also brought forth life?* she considered. Moab's religion taught so, and to her knowledge the Hebrews also believed that their ancestress, Eve, was mother of all living.

The funeral had been several days ago, now. This afternoon Ruth sat silent at the bedroom window from which she and Mahlon had often gazed across the Kir-Hareseth rooftops.

She could visualize her husband clearly, as though he breathed beside her, but the shock of his death still gripped her emotions in a stranglehold.

She was glad that during this period she was for-

bidden to wash, to anoint herself, to perform any
work, or even to put on shoes. Had she been required
to do any of these things, she could not have complied. The walk to the grave had been enough.

But, according to tradition, even the "stages" of
mourning were to be labeled. The day of the funeral
the widows were to be *'onen,'* the "sorrowing ones,"
whose sorrow was ordained, they were told, by God.
The seven days following the burial were for "deep
mourning," the first three called the "days of weeping." And during the entire week, they were to be
'avel,' the "bowed down," or "fading ones." This
depression, they were told, was encumbent upon
them, enjoined by the elders of Israel.

It was the end of the week, however, and Ruth had
yet to express the break within her own heart.

Doubtless her cold silence had not gone unnoticed
by her Jewish neighbors. Probably they considered it
evidence that a "pagan" cannot feel true love and loss.

Ruth knew better. Twice in her life she had lost,
and twice she had reacted thus. If anyone were crippled, she reasoned, it was the Jews themselves.

The regimen of tradition seemed, to her Moabite
eyes, to have stultified the very soul of their human
instinct. So prescribed were all their "good works"
that even the commonest courtesies were often devoid
of genuine feeling.

Everything ran on a proverb, it seemed. Ruth
would never forget the words of the rabbi who had
been their first caller:

"Whoever visits the widow takes away a sixtieth
part of her suffering," he had said, as he bowed
through the door. "To visit the brokenhearted takes

precedence over all other good works."

Ruth could not help but notice Naomi's strained smile as she graciously acknowledged his "kindness."

And then the funeral meal, provided by the nearby community, had smacked of duty in every course. Like the Passover supper, it had fit a perfect model. Bread, hard-boiled eggs, and lentils were the staples, each symbolic of some aspect of life and death, far beyond Ruth's retention. The only thing she remembered of the ordeal was Naomi's explanation that the food would consist alternately of round and coarse fare: "Round like life," she had said, "which is *rolling* unto death, the coarsest end."

No more than ten cups were to be emptied at this affair, two before the meal, five during, and three after, and all was to be served in the starkest earthenware.

The "service" thus accomplished, the three widows were left to a string of silent days, interrupted by countless visitors, each, in turn, determined to lift a "sixtieth" of their sorrow.

Ruth had once told Mahlon she could never be an Israelite. Now more than ever she felt this was true.

A large part of her still longed to be a "proper Jewess." But could the human heart be regimented, as they said it should? Why must everything be experienced by a formula?

Ruth knew she grieved, but not according to the precepts of tradition. Her heart had broken more surely than by prescription.

If she did not weep, it was not for lack of feeling, but for preponderence of it.

Rising from the window, Ruth walked to the bed

where she and Mahlon had spent countless nights of pleasure. She glanced down at the rip in the neckline of her undergarment, the handbreath seam which, by tradition, she was not to mend for thirty days.

Suddenly she relived the moment when Mahlon had first come to the weavery, his maroon cloak torn in much the same way.

There was no talented weaver who would patch the tear in her soul, as Tebit had cured the cloak. And there was no fuller who could cleanse away her misery.

With an empty sigh she lay back on the bed, drawing Mahlon's pillow to her breast. She remembered the warmth of his breath, and at last, the tears flowed.

CHAPTER
TEN

Thirty days after Mahlon's death Ruth worked a fine needle through the rip of her tunic's neckline.

She knew that the act of repairing the tear in the undergarment, the most intimate apparel, was supposed to symbolize a healing of grief. But Ruth's heart seemed beyond mending, her soul torn irreparably.

"Just another prescription," she muttered as she bent over the thin fabric which her father had woven months before.

She had not been surprised when Tebit and Marta were absent from the funeral procession. The ways of Judaism depressed them. Both parents had spent time at their daughter's side since Mahlon's death, however, urging her to return home and assuring her that all they possessed was at her disposal, if only she would do so.

To return to Tebit's house would be a perfectly natural thing, she realized. It was, in fact, expected of widows in Palestine and Transjordan that they would retreat to the shelter of their father's home—or to the security of the nearest male relation, had their father passed away.

But Ruth could not imagine going back to the weavery, and all it represented.

For, indeed, it *did* represent more than home and family, more than the house of her childhood. It represented a return to Chemosh. And though she had never announced a formal break with that religion, her spirit was farther from it than she dared admit.

Truly, Mahlon's analysis, the day he asked to be her suitor, had been correct: "Your heart left Chemosh long ago."

Still, there was much she did not understand of Judaism. She had sensed a growing hardness in herself regarding it as the period of mourning had progressed, and as the peculiar Hebrew folk had come and gone through Naomi's house. Panic gripped her when she realized this, for, hard as it was to acknowledge her depleted faith in Chemosh, it was more frightening to doubt Mahlon's way.

Though Ruth was not yet a proselyte, Judaism had been her link with hope, and to be confronted with its human flaws had brought a pall of despair such as she had never known.

As a wave of dread consumed her, the needle jerked in her grasp, and with a prick of pain, embedded itself beneath one of her nails. Wincing, she withdrew it and cradled the throbbing fingertip between her lips.

When a knock was heard at the door, she was ill-prepared to answer it, and even less eager to visit with the one whom Naomi scurried forth to admit. The matron, having just emerged from the kitchen, wiped her hands on her apron and bowed quietly to the rabbi, who was making his fourth call this week on the grieving widows.

Orpah remained in her room, apparently no more anxious than Ruth to endure the teacher's platitudes.

The dark-robed rabbi took a seat beside Naomi's fountain, graciously receiving her offer of mint tea. And, as he did so, he gave Ruth a tolerant smile.

"Shalom," he greeted her.

"Shalom, Rabbi," she returned.

"It is a pleasant afternoon, this last day of your mourning," he said, studying the sunlit heavens above the open court.

Ruth grimaced. "Pleasant enough," she acknowledged. "But it is *not* my last day of mourning."

The rabbi considered this, and then agreed. "Certainly, your heart will feel grief for the night, but joy comes with the dawn," he counseled.

"What dawn?" the girl inquired. "I see nothing but blackness ahead."

Naomi was surprised, upon bringing forth the tea, to find the Moabitess engaged in conversation with the teacher of Israel. Quietly she set her tray on the fountain bench and sat down.

"It must seem so, now," the rabbi commented. "But you are young. Much lies before you which will heal your anguish."

Ruth scrutinized the old fellow's wizened cheeks and furrowed brow. She had always been impressed by the dramatic effect of his trailing white beard against the stark black of his robe.

"And what of Mahlon, sir?" she inquired, not without a bitter tinge to her voice. "What lies ahead for him?"

"What do you mean?" the teacher asked, startled by her forthrightness.

At this Ruth gathered up her mending and approached him, sitting at his feet.

"Your people are divided on the matter," she pointed out. "Some say that Mahlon was apostate. Others," and she glanced at Naomi, "others know he was a righteous man."

The elder widow smiled shyly. Of course she had not always agreed with her son, nor with his father. But she did know that ultimately both were men of God, and she was curious as to how the rabbi would judge them.

Ruth leaned close to the master's knee and studied his face intently.

"Well," he stammered, "if you are asking about Mahlon's eternal soul. . . ."

"I am," she insisted.

"That is in Jehovah's hands," he hedged.

The matron watched with tense silence as her daughter-in-law pursued the subject.

"This is always the response you Israelites make to hard questions," the girl spurred him. "Now, good sir, what in truth is *your* opinion?"

The rabbi turned to Naomi, expecting her to correct her kinswoman's forwardness. But, to Ruth's delight, the elder woman only glanced away.

The master cleared his throat, rubbing his hands upon his robe.

"Teachers of Israel have many thoughts on the nature of the afterlife," he began at last. "They believe there are seven compartments each in paradise and hell, created before the world began, and the two are separated by just a handbreadth. On dying, only the perfect enter heaven at once."

The Moabitess shook her head, asking as reverently as possible, "But who is perfect? Have you ever met such a person?"

"A man is righteous by good works and by study of the Law," he continued, looking past her. "Notorious law-breakers and heretics have no hope whatever."

Ruth sighed. "And what of those who are neither perfect nor wholly evil?" she inquired. "Is there hope for them?"

"Some elders maintain," the rabbi replied, as though from rote, "that there is a purgatory through which such souls must pass for cleansing."

The questioner shuddered, her eyes burning. "A place of fire?" she asked, her voice rising more than she wished. "If so, how is your religion different from that of Chemosh?"

Naomi read the tension in the girl's fists, and wondered at her animosity.

As for the teacher, his reaction was predictable enough. "Young lady!" he rebuked her. "How dare you speak thus in your husband's home, and before a man of God?"

"I want to know," she cried, "if Mahlon is in torment! Have I lost him, as I lost my little brother, to the cruelty of another Chemosh?"

Naomi started, troubled at Ruth's frantic appeal. "Child," she marveled, "of what do you speak?"

The younger widow's face was white, her body rigid. "I had a brother," she managed, "who was sacrificed on the altar of Moab!"

The rabbi drew back, aghast, his hand raised to his heart. But quickly Naomi knelt with the girl, cradling her head upon her shoulder.

As Ruth wept, years of sorrow and pain flooding through her, the old woman wept as well.

Not caring whether the teacher would approve her theology, she said, "Cry, my dear child. Let the sadness go. Your little brother was an innocent, and your husband a friend of God. All lovers of Jehovah share in the world to come."

CHAPTER
ELEVEN

After the traditional month of mourning had passed, the three women of Naomi's house faced the question of how to manage their futures. Though the two brothers had succeeded in amassing a small savings, the estates of Mahlon and Chilion were limited, indeed.

Ruth walked today with Orpah among the booths of Kir-Hareseth's bazaar, gesturing emphatically, her brow furrowed.

"But, we owe it to Naomi!" she was saying. "Our mother-in-law has no one to whom she can turn. In weeks she will be destitute!"

Orpah, chin raised, eyed her sister-in-law narrowly. We *owe* her? What has she done but criticize and demean us since we married her sons? *I* owe her nothing!"

Ruth did not relate the incident of her talk with the rabbi, but shook her head. "You do not know her so well," she objected. "There is a gentle side to Naomi. A very tender side."

"Hmph," Orpah snorted. "I know you two have been cozy. But that proves nothing. She has never treated *me* decently at all!"

Ruth sighed and fumbled with a pile of pomegranates stacked on a merchant's bench. "Perhaps you have never given her reason to feel kindly toward you," she offered.

The tall woman displayed a typically offended expression. "Why do you side with her?" she snapped. "I tire of this!" And with a huff, she turned on her heel.

Seeing that she defeated her own purpose, Ruth quickly followed. "Orpah," she called, her hand outstretched, "we have been companions a long time. Do this for me. Besides," she reasoned, grasping her arm, "you do not wish to return to your parents, do you?"

Chilion's slender widow pivoted hesitantly, her hard face softening. "All right, Ruth. You have always been a 'woman's friend,' as your name implies. I will hear your case. But," she added, "for you only—not for Naomi!"

The petitioner smiled and squeezed Orpah's arm affectionately. "Then, listen," she began. "This is my plan. . . ."

Orpah had never contributed to her father's dye trade. She had spent her youth at her mother's knee, and with the party-goers of Kir-Hareseth. Therefore, it was agreed that the two young widows would use Ruth's knowledge of textiles to bring revenue into Naomi's coffers.

They were determined to see to it, despite Orpah's ill feelings, that their mother-in-law was provided for.

Tebit was approached, and an arrangement made whereby the two ladies would manage his booth on market day in exchange for a small commission on goods sold. The advantage to Ruth's father would be in free time to work at the weavery during bazaar hours.

Through the winter and into spring the women labored in this way, but as it turned out, Tebit's wares were forced to compete with the attention Orpah drew from male passersby. More often than not, a cluster of wolf-eyed men dominated the space before the booth, spending the beauty's energy in idle conversation and rowdy flirtation.

Orpah did little to dissuade such attentions, and each day matters grew more out of hand, until Ruth was embarrassed to accompany her sister-in-law.

At last, Mahlon's widow objected. "People will think this a booth of solicitation!" she murmured one day.

"A what?" the tall one cried.

"Truly, Orpah. When is enough enough?" Ruth demanded. "I fear for our reputation. We have sold only two small swatches today. We waste our time, and my father's!"

In frustration, Ruth gathered up her lunch satchel and headed for home, Orpah following her anxiously.

"I am sorry!" she shouted. "Can I help it if men are drawn to me?"

"Yes," Ruth replied flatly. "There are more important things for now."

Orpah pursued her friend to Naomi's front door, where both came to a sudden halt, trying to interpret what their eyes told them.

Three small donkey carts, half full of goods from the old widow's home, sat before the entryway. Women from Naomi's Jewish community shuffled in and out of the house, carrying piles of linens and kitchenware, tears brimming in their eyes as they deposited the possessions in the wagons.

"What are you doing?" Ruth barked. "Where is our mother-in-law?"

No one seemed inclined to answer the question, as the matrons muttered among themselves and shook their heads.

Pushing past them, Ruth left Orpah outside and ran into the courtyard, calling for Naomi.

When the elder woman entered the gallery, the girl was relieved but disconcerted.

"What is happening?" she demanded, dashing up the stairs. "What are these people doing?"

"I did not expect you to return so early," Naomi stammered. "Did things go well at the bazaar?"

Ruth noticed the widow's red-rimmed eyes, and her own heart beat anxiously. "You have been crying, Mother? Tell me, what is this madness?" she implored, gesturing to the packed crates and stacks of clothing strewn on the patio floor.

"I would have waited till evening," Naomi assured her. "I would never have gone without seeing you first."

"Go?" Ruth cried. "You are going? But where . . . ?"

Naomi descended the stairs and went to the fountain bench, sitting there calmly. "I have thought about it for days," she explained, her hands resting in her lap. "It is best for all of us if I return to Bethlehem."

"But. . . ."

"But nothing," she said firmly. "The famine in Israel passed years ago. When Elimelech brought us here, it was to stay only until we could safely return.

I have people there," she insisted, "and a small plot of land. I can grow barley on the field."

Ruth, who had now been joined by Orpah, stared in amazement at the old woman.

"You cannot be serious!" she exclaimed. "Orpah, do you hear her?"

The other daughter-in-law only shook her head, rolling her eyes as though to question the elder's sanity.

"Mother," Ruth continued, ignoring Orpah's insinuation, "even if you could endure such a journey, it is too late to plant barley. In fact the harvest will begin shortly. You could have no income until a later season, if you could even manage such a new vocation. What do you know of farming?" Ruth implored. "Please, think!"

Naomi focused offended eyes on Mahlon's widow. "God will care for me," she reasoned. "I believe it is time for me to return."

Ruth sighed, fearing that she was losing ground. And then a new approach struck her. "Passover!" she cried. "It shall soon be Passover again. If Jehovah wished for you to make such a journey, it would not be during your most holy of festivals!"

But the matron would not be undone. "How could a Jew honor Passover more than to be returning to the Promised Land?" she argued. "That, after all, is what the celebration commemorates—the liberation of our people from heathen bondage!"

Ruth shook her head in exasperation. "You are not fair!" she declared, an angry edge in her voice. "Always you pull religion out of your sleeve, as though common sense were of no value."

131

The mother-in-law studied the cloud-strewn sky and, for a moment, Ruth thought she had lost her completely.

"There is little left of your funds, Mother," she pleaded. "Tell me, how will you survive? And where will you find strength for such a life in a new land?"

Suddenly, Naomi stared at Ruth full-faced, a chuckle rising from her throat. "New land?" she repeated. "Israel *is* my land! As old as Jacob's bones, and running deep through my blood as the Jordan through El Ghor! 'If I forget thee, O Israel, let my right hand forget her cunning,' " she recited, lifting her palms to the sky. " 'If I forget. . . .' "

Ruth grasped her wrist in one last attempt to shake her into reality. But it was no use. The old woman was obviously determined, and sat rigid on the bench.

Then, matter-of-factly, she arose, inquiring of the Jewish women who had come to help, "Is it almost ready?"

One matron, dabbing her eyes with her sleeve, nodded, saying, "Only what you see on the pavement is left to be loaded."

"Good," Naomi said smiling. "The gallery rooms are all clear, and so, I shall be going with the next merchant train."

Turning for the door, she rapidly set the matter out. "I would have left this evening, but since my girls have already returned, I can seek an earlier passage. I will attach myself to the spice-merchant's caravan which is due to pass this way shortly."

Ruth eyed the swollen money bag on Naomi's belt. She would be spending nearly all her resources to

pay for the train's protection through the wilds of
Moab and Jordan.

One hundred miles and many days of travel lay
ahead for the old woman. Ruth shuddered.

"Mother!" she cried as the matron gathered up her
cloak and helped load the remaining parcels into the
little carts. "Is there nothing I can say to dissuade
you?"

The elder widow stopped at the portal and studied
her daughter-in-law compassionately. Then, without
a word, she proceeded to the task.

One last item remained to be carried to the
wagons. Elimelech's shrouded potting wheel sat near
the door. Naomi bent over it fondly, lifting it in her
arms like a child, and placing it beside her own seat
in the front cart. Then, standing guard, she awaited
the merchant's caravan.

Ruth's heart pounded. Turning to Orpah, she
whispered firmly, "Prepare for a journey, sister. We
are going with her!"

Orpah stared, incredulous, into Ruth's fiery eyes.
"Are you *also* mad?" she muttered through
clenched teeth. "Why should we leave Moab?"

"Because," the girl insisted, "she needs us."

"Ha!" Orpah smirked, studying Naomi covertly.
"She may need *you,* but for me she has no use."

"She has more use for both of us than she can
imagine," Ruth argued. "With no one to care for her,
she may die before reaching Israel. Do you want that
on your conscience?"

The tall one sighed, her head spinning. Still Ruth
continued her defense, using the same reasoning with
which she had won her partnership in the bazaar.

"Everything you have in this world was given you by Naomi's youngest son. Yet your parents will never let you forget your poverty. If you return to them, they will choose your next husband, without regard to your wishes. Is that what you want?"

Orpah's mind was clouded with conflict. Her sister-in-law spoke the truth and yet she wondered if she would fare any better in a foreign land.

But Ruth allowed no time to weigh the matter. Taking Orpah by the arm, she led her into the house and up the gallery steps.

Calling for Naomi's friends, she asked for additional crates and satchels. "We have more for you to load," she explained. "We will accompany our lady to Bethlehem."

CHAPTER
TWELVE

Except for Ruth's journey with Mahlon to the marketplace of Ar, neither sister-in-law had ever left Kir-
Hareseth. For each, the "city of pottery" was the
world, and though it sat on the King's Highway trade
route, whatever lay beyond was a fantasy which they
rarely contemplated.

The mammoth gates of Moab's capital were a
common sight to the two women who had been born
beneath their shadow. But today, the giant doors took
on an awesome aspect, symbolizing all their nation
and culture meant to them.

For the gates were the boundaries of their home.
To pass through them with no intention of returning
was enough to shake the most courageous soul. And
though the women's destination was not far distant, it
was such a departure spiritually that the prospect
must not be dwelt on.

For Ruth, the thought of life in Israel brought
mixed feelings, just as marriage to an Israelite had set
up a challenge which she had found both exhilarating
and baffling.

For Orpah, there was no attraction. Conscience,
the fear of returning to parents who would scorn her
previous choices, and the influence of Mahlon's
widow had tipped the scales. But now, as the reality

of her decision set in, with the looming city gates, she trembled.

Naomi, who rode beside Ruth on the seat of the first wagon, repeatedly glanced at Orpah, who graced the tailgate, her sandaled feet dangling like lost children over the edge.

"I wish you would both reconsider," the mother-in-law pleaded. "There is really no need to uproot yourselves for my sake."

Orpah looked longingly at Ruth, but the young widow paid no heed.

"We are your only family," the girl objected. "We have made our decision."

But Naomi was unconvinced.

"See here," she pointed to the side of the viaduct, "the very grove in which you used to play with your little brother. How can you turn your back on all that is precious?"

Orpah, too, scanned the familiar streets and house fronts, remembering the many parties she had enjoyed in Kir-Hareseth, and the attentions she had always received from its men.

Ignoring Orpah's pout, however, Ruth set her shoulders squarely. "The temple of Chemosh looms above everything here," she reminded Naomi. "I can no longer dwell beneath its spirit."

Naomi marveled at the girl's firm resolve, but, looking again at Orpah, inquired, "And what of your friend? I doubt she is like-minded."

Ruth did not reply, only studied the colossal gates beneath which the wagons now passed. When they had reached the other side, however, the mother had come to a decision of her own.

Calling to the caravan master, she asked that he stop the train.

The old fellow, wondering already if he had been wise to accept these female passengers, nodded grumpily and ordered his servants to a halt.

Naomi, full of authority, descended and went to the back of the cart, where she found Orpah choking back inner turmoil.

The moment the matron confronted her, tears began to well in the girl's eyes, and for the first time since Orpah had joined her family, Naomi embraced her.

"Go," the mother-in-law insisted, speaking to both young widows. "Return, each of you, to her mother's house. May the Lord deal kindly with you as you have dealt with the dead . . . and with me."

Instantly, Ruth left her side of the wagon and ran to the elder, grasping her close and shaking her head emphatically.

"May the Lord grant that you may find rest," Naomi went on, "with new husbands."

"No!" Ruth cried.

But the matron only returned her embrace and, drawing both women to herself, kissed each on the forehead.

Immediately the two girls began to weep, their voices raised in a chorus of grief and confusion.

"No!" Ruth cried again, as Naomi stepped away. "We will surely return with you to your people!"

The other Moabitess, overcome with an admixture of emotions, found herself nodding agreement.

But Naomi took an insistent stance. "Go back, my daughters," she commanded, her voice broken with the weight of her own feelings. "Why should you return with me? Have I yet sons in my womb, that they may be your husbands?"

"Return, my daughters," she repeated, pointing toward the city. "Go! For I am too old to have a husband. Why, even if I should have a husband tonight and bear sons again, would you wait until they were grown? Would you refrain from marrying?"

Here she paused, a sad twinkle lighting her old eyes, as though she was pleased with her own wry humor.

But the tension did not ease, and when she could restrain her tears no longer, she averted her gaze, trying to conceal her heart.

"No, my daughters," she wept, "this is harder for me than for you, for the hand of the Lord has gone forth against me."

This declaration was more than her young listeners could receive, and again they raised their voices in weeping.

But it was Orpah who made the first move. Unable to bear the heaviness another moment, and knowing that she only prolonged the inevitable, she followed her original desires.

Approaching Naomi, whose back was to her, she put her arms around the stooped shoulders and bent forward, kissing the matron's weathered cheek.

Then, with a quiet groan, she walked quickly back toward town, not daring to look Ruth in the eye.

Mahlon's widow observed the departure numbly. But with the abandonment, a jolt of urgency moved her, and like a desperate child she clung to Naomi, holding her tight, and weeping upon her neck.

"Never shall I leave you!" she declared.

"Oh, my dear girl," Naomi cried, a tumult of sorrow, "behold, your sister-in-law has gone back to her people and her gods. Go with her, Ruth!"

But the Moabitess—the one who had doubted Chemosh long ago, who had hung between two cultures and two commitments, winning the love and trust of a Jewess's eldest son and the hesitant heart of his mother—would not be dissuaded.

Looking into Naomi's eyes, her own full of tears, she petitioned, "Where would I go and what would I do without you, Mother? Do not urge me to leave you or to turn from following after you. For where you go, I will go, and where you lodge I will lodge. Your people shall be my people . . . and your God, my God."

The matron stared at her, incredulous, wondering if she knew the import of her own words. But Ruth was more than aware, and pledging a lifelong trust, she fervently vowed, "Where you die, I will die, and there will I be buried. Thus may the Lord do to me, and worse, if anything but death parts you and me."

PART III
Growth

How blessed is the one whose strength is in thee;
In whose heart are the highways of Zion!

PSALM 84:5

This one is like a tree firmly planted by streams of
   water,
Which yields its fruit in its season.

PSALM 1:3
A Psalm of David
(Author's paraphrase)

CHAPTER
ONE

Upward from Kir-Hareseth, to Dibon and Heshbon, the spice merchant's caravan wended. It skirted the northern edge of the Dead Sea through the Plains of Moab, and would finally cross the famed boundary separating Israel from all points east—the sluggish Jordan River.

Except for her first glimpse of the Wadi Mojib and the rampant Arnon which slit the gorge with a violent streak, Ruth would have little reason to recall her passage through the barren Moab terrain. Only one night about the campfire would stay with her.

They were somewhere in the depths of the desert just before the gorge, the train having pulled into the traditional circle which would give its passengers a form of security through the dark hours. Naomi and Ruth sat alone to one side of the fire, while the crew who managed the caravan sat on the other, laughing and joking in rowdy conversation.

The wagon master had seen to it that the women were treated tolerably well, their only discomfort being the occasional leering smiles or obscene remarks directed their way when he was not looking. For this, they had been as prepared as any two females might be, having dwelt in a man's world all their lives. And the merchant who protected them did so only because it was his duty as their paid guide.

Ruth wondered if the brethren of Judah would be any kinder. "Mother," she said, for the first time considering her future, "do women fare well in Israel?"

The matron knew she contemplated the men across the fire, and answered with reserve. "I should like to think so," she replied. "The Laws of Moses defend us well. But still, we must beware. For not every Israelite is a gentleman."

Ruth was surprised by Naomi's honesty, the woman who lived for the very breezes of Palestine.

"In all, however," the elder added, "I think you will do well . . . if you do not grieve for your own country."

Ruth pulled away and looked at her intently. "I told you that your land would be my land!" she affirmed.

Naomi stared into the desert shadows. "You did, my dear. Forgive me. But . . . "

Ruth listened closely.

" . . . what of your parents?" the matron asked. "You never bade them good-bye. How your mother must be sorrowing just now!"

The girl stiffened, a lump forming in her throat. "In their way, my parents have loved me," she acknowledged. "But only in their way. They could not give me more than Chemosh—and Chemosh I abhor."

Naomi nodded respectfully, again amazed at the girl's resolve. "I suppose Orpah will have told them of your going," she said.

"Indeed."

"And if they wish to contact you, it is not impossible."

Ruth perceived the struggle Naomi experienced as she empathized with the parents' loss.

"Certainly, they may," she assured her. "But I do not expect it. My father is a proud man, and my mother lives beneath his shadow. I will pray for them, and remember them always. But you are my family now."

The names of Tebit and Marta would never pass between them again.

The light of the fire was reflected in small yellow orbs which peeked here and there from the camp's wilderness border. But no wild creature approached the caravan. Only the distant cry of a desert owl echoed the laughter of the crewmen, and life in Moab would be behind them tomorrow.

Compared to the Arnon, Jordan was a boring trickle, slipping wearily through the arid waste which marked its entrance into the Salt Sea. Were this not the boundary divorcing her finally from her old life and delineating the new, Ruth would have had no reason to notice it.

As for Naomi, both rivers moved her emotions. Upon crossing Arnon, it seemed she was freed of a great burden, the land of captivity slipping off her like invisible shackles. And the sight of Jordan brought tears to her eyes, a lilt to her spirits.

It was not until about three-quarters of the way into the ten-day journey, when the caravan reached the outskirts of the ruins called "Jericho," that Ruth sat up attentively. Here she could begin to appreciate what beauty lay on this greener side of El Ghor.

The colors of Moab were those of the desert which painted a wonder all its own. But never could it rival the heady hues she saw before her. Flaming "fire-trees," once cultivated here for their ornamental foliage, still grew wild among the abandoned rubble of the once mighty city, and their contrast with the verdant splendor of surrounding vegetation especially awed her.

Far more awesome than the area's native glory, however, was the history of the city's overthrow. Every Palestinian and Transjordanian knew the tale of the Hebrews' victory over Jericho, and the apparently miraculous intervention of their God, as their leader Joshua confronted the walled metropolis.

The Israelites had never waged war against the folk of Jericho. It was the first town to face them as they entered the Holy Land bent on conquest, and its broad wall simply crumbled before them, as if it were a string of toy blocks leveled by some invisible giant's fist.

The incident had served as an object lesson for Israel's enemies ever since, and as a reminder to Jew and Gentile alike of the nation's supernatural origins.

Ruth knew the story well. However, seeing the heap of destruction firsthand strengthened her, as never before, in her new faith.

Beyond Jericho lay the range whose western slope led down to the "Great Sea," one day to be called "Mediterranean." And at its pinnacle, fifteen steep miles from the ruins, sat the stoutly fortified city of Jebus—ancient Salem, one day to be called "Jeru-Salem." Past this point the wilderness and the desert gave way to the balmy air and greener pastures of Judea. The Moabites, as Ruth and Mahlon had discussed, were a shepherd race. But their grazing lands were not comparable to those of this province.

The entire trip, though free of bandit raids and un-threatened by wild beasts, should have tired a woman of Naomi's age. Instead, it seemed to have infused her with long-dormant vigor. And when they began the five-mile descent from Jebus toward her home-town, she tingled with anticipation, her old eyes scanning the region along the road, as each bend, each dip evoked a memory.

"We are very near!" she whispered repeatedly. "It will not be long now."

Ruth took her thin hand and held it close, listening as she recounted the short journeys she had made in her youth upon this very highway.

"Watch carefully now," she said, pointing to a little rise some distance ahead. "When we come nearer that hill, you will see a tower, the 'Migdal Eder,' which marks the boundary of Bethlehem!"

" 'Tower of the flock,' " Ruth interpreted. "What is its purpose?"

"From it the herdsmen watch over the sheep who are destined for sacrifice in our Tabernacle," Naomi explained.

"Is that like Moab's temple?" Ruth inquired. "Do you worship there?"

Again, as always, Naomi chafed at drawing any comparison between her religion and that of Chemosh. But she replied as kindly as possible.

"It holds a similar function, though it is nothing like Kir-Hareseth's mighty building," she said. "Our Tabernacle is a great tent, with wooden walls and a cloth roof. For splendor it cannot rival the palaces of heathen gods. But," she asserted, "it houses the Glory of Jehovah—the Shechinah itself!"

Ruth considered this carefully, wondering how to phrase the questions which the image provoked.

"Mother," she marveled, "if Jehovah is God of all the earth and King of all creation, does he not deserve the very finest of resting places? Why is he content to dwell in a tent?"

Naomi was not offended by the question. It was to be expected that the neophyte would wonder at the seeming incongruity.

"The Tabernacle is, as the name implies, only a temporary dwelling place. One day, we all dream, there will be a magnificent palace for our King. But our people have been pilgrims on the earth for generations. Only three hundred years ago did we enter Canaan. And we have yet to rise above our nomadic roots."

Naomi paused, and Ruth knew, from experience, that when the old woman got that faraway look, she wished not to speak for a while.

Still, the girl desired to know more.

"Where is your Tabernacle?" she asked. "I would have expected to see it in a hilltop city . . . like Jebus."

Naomi smiled, nodding. "Of course—we all wish for that! What could be a more magnificent setting? But that town is still ruled by the Jebusites, and though our people have settled all about it, taming the land in each direction, the great fortress bears a heathen name.

"And so," she went on, "we settle for having our Tabernacle several miles north, near Shechem, at a place called Shiloh. But," she said raising a gnarled finger, "not for long!"

The old woman's eyes twinkled, as if with some secret. "Jebus was originally called Salem, and its king was Melchizedek, who blessed our father Abraham. To this mighty one Abraham offered a tenth of his spoils. Do you remember?"

Ruth thought back to the stories she had learned in childhood. "Yes, I recall this tale," she said. "It was after he rescued our father Lot from the Mesopotamian confederacy." Her eyes grew wistful, as she remembered how she and Mahlon had discussed that very tale in their journey across the plain to Ar. "The king of Salem was a mysterious character, was he not?" she added.

"Indeed—for his throne was established by God himself. Does this not tell you something?"

The young Moabitess dwelt on this some moments, appreciation for her newly adopted faith infusing her. How deep it was! And how profound!

She looked over her shoulder at the retreating crest upon which the walls of Jebus could still be discerned.

Of course that city was meant for the children of Isaac! It made perfect sense.

CHAPTER
TWO

Once the Migdal Eder came into view, its rough, rocky sides rising conelike above the landscape, the expanse of countryside seemed suddenly to blossom with activity.

It was the beginning of barley harvest as Naomi and Ruth approached the old home territory. Acres of creamy white grain on tall, slender stalks demanded attention from the countless reapers who dotted the fields.

A warm breeze wafted up toward the Olivet range, causing the horizon to undulate like the sea, and the workers plied their tasks quickly while heat of day lingered. As much grain as possible must be brought in before moist evening air saturated the stalks, making them tough and sickle-resistant.

New life was everywhere, small white lambs skittering through the chartreuse meadows.

And then it came into full view, the tiny realm of Bethlehem.

Larger than a village, it did not qualify as a town, for it was neither populous enough nor fortified sufficiently. It met the specifications of a "township," having a low wall and a gate, where the elders convened for purposes of fellowship and judicial decision. But there were so many villages and townships in Palestine, that such a place would never merit much fame or recognition. And Bethlehem was among the least in Judah.

Had it not been for its strategic location, about one-third of the way on the road from Jebus to Hebron, it would have dwindled to a ghost town long ago. As it was, enough commerce passed through, that the little city survived on more than agrarian pursuits.

There were, in fact, a few wealthy residents. Ruth could see this, as the caravan wound down the last slope leading toward the white-walled burg. Along the hill against which the town rested were some very fine homes, pristine and gleaming beneath the spring sun.

As dusk descended, she was entranced by their pale pink reflection. Leaning close to her mother-in-law, she whispered, "What sort of folk dwell there?"

Naomi followed Ruth's gaze. "Merchants, owners of the grain fields . . . those who had enough in store to make it through the famine. Some of them are kin to Elimelech, but they never left Judah."

A sadness overtook her at the thought of those lean years. But she turned her attention to the road.

"Stop here!" she called to the caravan master. "We will be leaving you now."

Naomi had paid for the merchant's protection, half in advance, and now was to pay the rest. The old fellow halted his train, and dismounting from his horse, walked to the matron's cart.

Holding out a grizzled hand, he took the coins she offered — the last ones in her purse — and bowed congenially.

"Never been through your little town," he commented. "Passed by here many times going to Hebron and points south."

"Then," the widow returned, "you have missed something! Bethlehem has a fine market."

The caravaneer nodded kindly, but looked unconvinced. "Well," he said with a nod, "I must take it in sometime."

Then, grasping the harness of Naomi's little donkey, he directed her three vehicles to the highway shoulder, where a narrower road led down toward the hamlet.

"Will you be returning to Moab soon?" he inquired.

The Jewess's face crinkled in a broad smile. "Not in my lifetime!" she replied.

CHAPTER
THREE

Dusk was descending as Naomi and Ruth passed
under the town gate and approached the central court
of Bethlehem.

The women of the little city were just emerging
from their homes to make their second daily journey
to the fountain adorning the square. Since the coolest
hours were at early morning and evening, these were
the traditional times—not only for the filling of water
jugs—but for conversation.

Naomi, who had experienced such joy at entering
the town, now pulled her little train over to the side
of the plaza, and watched the activity in tense silence. Though she sat very still, her bearing was
rigid—and Ruth knew her thoughts.

"Do you remember any of these women?" she
asked.

Naomi did not take her eyes from the growing
crowd, but sighed, "Oh, my dear girl, I know every
one of them! Bethlehem is very small, you see."

"Yes, Mother." The girl smiled. "Then you remember their names. Why not present yourself?"

The widow of Elimelech studied their contented
pace and lingered over the children who played between their skirts. Passing a veined hand over her
cheek, she shook her head. "How little they have
changed!" she exclaimed. "Except that the small ones

now would be their grandchildren, and not their own sons and daughters." Trembling, she sighed again. "I recognize them all!" she marveled. "Dorca there, and Rebekkah . . . and over there, by the willow, Sara and Tamara. Oh, Ruth, they will never know me!"

The Moabitess was perplexed. "Why, Mother? How could they have forgotten you?"

"I do not doubt that they would remember the wife of Bethlehem's finest potter," she whispered proudly. "But," she said, shaking her head once more, "they would never dream I had grown so old!"

Ruth's eyes were wide and she took Naomi's hand. "Now, lady, you exaggerate! You are a fine woman. Fine, indeed!"

Her commendation would soon be tested, as the square was populated with an increasing crowd of females. It was inevitable that the newcomers would be noticed, and it was not chance that a relative was the first to do so.

A plump bundle of energy, Abigail had not altered, except to gain a few pounds, since Naomi had last seen her. The instant the matron of Moab observed her kinswoman, she crouched down on the wagon seat.

"Oh, no!" Naomi exclaimed. "If she follows her old ways, she will be offering our donkey a drink of water, whether we like it or not."

"Why, how kind!" Ruth laughed. "Indeed, she is coming this way. Who is she?"

"One of my cousins. Abigail prides herself on hospitality," the elder muttered. "Her house is by the city gate, and always she has made it a point to comfort strangers who wander into town. 'The first with the ladle,' they call her. Always there to water and feed the beasts of burden."

By now the portly Jewess was directly before Naomi's wagon, her hand on the donkey's muzzle, and her eyes bright with greeting.

"Good-day, ladies!" she bubbled. "You must have come down with the caravan. Did you join it in Jebus, or where?"

Her question was directed at the elder traveler, whom she assumed would be in charge of the three little carts. As Naomi did not answer promptly, however, Abigail glanced at Ruth, and her clear brown eyes quickly assessed that this younger lady was a foreigner.

"Ah!" She smiled. "You would be from beyond Jordan! Yes—you have traveled very far. You must be terribly weary."

With this she scuttled off to bring a draft of well water. Returning with a bucketful, she placed it before the donkey and laughed, raising her index finger with a wink. "The poor beasts first, and then my ladies."

Twice more she did this, providing Naomi's other burros with refreshment, and then hurried away for cups, that she might offer the two strangers the same.

Ruth was dazzled by her cheery energy, but Naomi withdrew further into silence until the woman returned.

When the self-appointed hostess reached out an ample hand, holding forth the cool offering, the old widow's heart broke. "Abigail," she said hoarsely.

The chubby face altered from one of sheer congeniality to one of bewilderment. Abigail's eyes no longer scanned the visitor as a stranger, but surveyed her closely, trying to identify the voice.

"Madam," she marveled, "you know my name?"

"Truly, cousin," the matron replied. "And you once knew me well."

Suddenly, the cobwebs of time were blown aside, and Abigail looked upon her kinswoman with full awareness.

"Naomi?" she cried. "Is that you?"

The widow could not speak, but only nodded, tears welling along her gray lashes.

With a rush of unspeakable feeling, Abigail drew alongside the wagon and embraced the sojourner. "Oh, my friend," she wept, "we had thought you long dead! We had given up hope of ever seeing you again!"

"Since the moment my feet left this soil," Naomi replied, "I *have* been as one dead."

Abigail held her tight, weeping on her shoulder, and then drew back, wiping her eyes. "So, Naomi," she said, trying to compose herself, "where is your family? Elimelech . . . your sons . . . and who is this beside you?"

But before the widow could respond, the neighbor women had left the well and converged upon the little cart. Questions buzzed, demanding satisfaction. "Friends, Abigail? Introduce us. Who are they? Do tell!"

As it happened with the kinswoman, so it happened with these old companions. One by one, their eyes were opened—some by the sound of Naomi's voice, some by her manner or the tilt of her chin. Gradually, they saw past the creases which years of frustration had worn into her brow, and they recognized the gentle spirit which peeked past the hardness protecting her soul.

"Naomi?" they marveled. "Is this Naomi?"

Soon a number of them had called their husbands, and weary men emerged from shady spots, where they rested from a hard day's labor. Younger fellows who had once been playmates of Mahlon and Chilion spoke with the elders in whispers, and again the questions came. "Can this be Naomi? Our brother Elimelech and his sons—will they be coming? Did it go well for the potter in Moab?"

But, at last, the old widow raised her hand, asking for silence, and a hush settled over the crowd.

"Call me not 'Naomi,' " she said, almost in rebuke. "Call me 'Mara.' For the Almighty has dealt very bitterly with me."

The elders leaned together with furrowed brows and the women murmured among themselves, until Abigail called them to attention. "Let her speak!" she commanded. And then, nodding to her cousin, she said, "Tell us, dear, how it fell out with you in Moab, and why you have returned alone."

The widow studied the reins which rested in her lap and fingered them sadly. "My husband has been dead five years, and my two sons passed away only months ago. Save for my daughter-in-law, I am alone in the world."

Here she stopped, unable to say more. And as the crowd contemplated her sad story, shrugging heads in helpless wonder or offering fruitless condolences, Ruth pressed close to the matron, drawing her head to her shoulder.

The loveliness of the young foreigner had escaped no one, and her selfless venture to Bethlehem would be the topic of conversation at many a dinner table that evening.

But Abigail would not allow her kinswoman to suffer further interrogation.

"Let them pass now," she called, for indeed the crowd had grown so great, the street was congested.

As the hostess led the little train away, she glanced at Naomi. "Surely you will stay with me tonight," the cousin insisted, her round face full of compassion.

The matron had not yet found her voice, and so Ruth answered for her. "You are very kind," she said, accepting the offer.

As the cart was led toward Abigail's gateside home, the masses parting, the mother-in-law at last found strength to raise her head. Calling over her shoulder, she soundly stated her condition once more. "Call me not 'Naomi,' " she repeated. "For I went out full and the Lord has brought me home again empty!"

The onlookers sensed the bitter edge in her tone, and had no words of comfort. As they watched the wagon depart the square, they could only sympathize with the widow's pain, and with the broken spirit she expressed.

"Why do you call me 'Naomi'?" she challenged again, her voice increasing with the distance. "Seeing that the Lord has testified against me, and the Almighty has afflicted me?"

CHAPTER
FOUR

Ruth rose, having slept little. She walked to the edge
of the rooftop, where Abigail had kindly offered lodg-
ing for the night.

In the deep of darkness, Bethlehem, unlike Kir-
Hareseth, was very still. Ruth was not used to such
quiet. In her home city, the night streets rang with
activity.

And she was not accustomed to the blackness, interrupted only by the spring moon. Kir-Hareseth was
well lit at all times.

Unfamiliar surroundings were not the only cause of
Ruth's restlessness, however. Beneath a small tentlike
awning, situated in the center of the roof, Naomi
rested. But Ruth could see, by her fitful turnings, that
if she slept, it was not soundly. And the daughter-in-
law sensed that the return to Bethlehem was inten-
sifying the matron's depression, rather than elevating
it.

She recalled with a shudder the widow's declaration this evening, proclaiming her misery before the
entire city.

"Call me not 'Naomi'!"

How quickly the twinkle of anticipation and the
glimmer of fresh life had been replaced by customary
bitterness!

The darkness, however, and the quiet, did add to

Ruth's own fears. If her mother-in-law were to deteriorate rather than revive—if Ruth were left to fend for herself in an alien country—where was Jehovah's hand?

There was no distraction in the streets below to forestall such morbid thoughts. No sound of traffic or noise of celebration interrupted her worst imaginings.

She wondered now, only days after making the most momentous decision of her life, if she had been a fool.

Crossing her arms, she grasped herself firmly by the shoulders and tried to think on pleasant things. But the only scenes to flash before her were of Mahlon and his tender smile; of Mahlon as he had once stood in their bedroom door, his mantle drawn prophetlike over his head; of Mahlon and his warm hands as they had wooed her in private moments.

A rush of grief flooded up from her heart, choking her and burning her eyes. Reflexively she reached for the rooftop rail and gripped it tightly, taking a constricted breath.

She tried frantically to recall Naomi's psalm—the one which had transformed the old woman's sorrow the day Ruth had witnessed her meditation.

But it was useless. Naomi never sang these days, and Ruth could not recall her refrains of faith.

Through a blur of tears she lifted her eyes to the gentle hills cradling the town. But even they reminded her of Mahlon, and his talks of his homeland.

As she perused the slopes, however, something caught her attention. Where the homes of the wealthy graced the hills, beyond which the shepherd fields lay silent, a soft light moved across someone's balcony.

Despite Ruth's consuming sorrow, she was drawn to study its golden glow.

It was a lantern, she determined, held by some other wakeful soul. She wondered who but herself would be troubled in this peaceful setting, and what thoughts might have roused him.

Back and forth the little lamp was carried, traversing the distant porch. And then it stopped its movement, being set to rest upon the balcony rail.

As she waited, watching, she saw a form draw close in the light's glowing circle. For a long moment the lampbearer stood beside the lantern, until he bent low above it, snuffing it out.

The distance between herself and that balcony was so great, she could tell little of the nature of the stranger, though by his size and bearing she knew he was indeed a man, and not a woman.

The dim light of the spring night took over where the lamp had faded, and she could still perceive that he stood upon his porch, his white robe caught softly by the harvest moon.

Though he turned to enter his chamber, she felt less isolation. Someone else in this foreign place was lonely. And that knowledge somehow eased her despair.

CHAPTER
FIVE

Naomi lifted the rusty key in shaky fingers and
stepped into the sunken entryway of her estate.

An ancient lock hanging in a web of dust and
spider tracks was all that stood between herself and
the host of haunting memories dwelling just beyond
the door.

Though for almost twelve years she had dreamed
of returning to this house and reclaiming her place in
Bethlehem, she had postponed the final leg of her
journey all morning.

When Abigail could not think of one more chore in
which to engage her old friend, and Naomi could not
dredge up another bit of conversation, the widow had
finally accepted the inevitable. She had come home,
not to rest at her cousin's house, but to renew her own
station.

It was Ruth, however, who gathered up the clothing
and toiletries they had taken to Abigail's rooftop, and
it was she who placed the bundles beside the hostess's
door.

"Come, Mother," she had insisted. "We must set up
before evening."

The home of Elimelech pleased the daughter-in-
law the instant she saw it. From Abigail's house it lay
several twists and turns away, upon one of the

quietest streets of the already-quiet town. In fact it backed against the low wall of the village, at the foot of the highlands which had attracted Ruth's interest only the night before.

But it was the building's serenity which most appealed to her. Nestled between several other housefronts, the pale stone of the estate was drab by comparison, having been neglected of whitewash since the owners had departed. This did not detract from its beauty, however. In fact, it added a quaint somberness to the place, as though it longed for attention.

A spring-green ivy clung to the portal and wound its way about the cracks and fissures of the home's facade, until it fairly cloaked the lintel. Leaves and debris from nearly a dozen winters encrusted the path to the door, and softened the sound of the women's steps upon the stone porch.

Ruth drew each breath carefully as Naomi fumbled with the lock, almost afraid to disturb the air.

When at last the creaking door was pushed open, it was upon a dank and musty corridor. Holding her mantle over her nose, Naomi led Ruth toward the afternoon light which marked the courtyard ahead.

The descending cool of early evening was spinning a carpet of leaves, dropped on the patio by countless autumn winds, raising its corners in frolics and its broad stretches in ripples. A waterless fountain stood silent and forlorn at the center, but as Ruth drew near it, disturbing the dust of many seasons with a swipe of her hand, she smiled broadly.

The little structure, which had once played liquid music, was made of pale pink marble, and she could imagine that, in its time, it had been a thing of beauty.

"Oh, Mother," she cried, "it is lovely! This will be our first project—to resurrect this piece of art."

Stepping back, she envisioned the sculpture cleaned and polished. But when she turned to Naomi, she found the old woman lost in remembrances, and wondered what thoughts made her lip quiver, her eyes mist.

While Ruth tried to imagine the tune of the fountain, the matron's ears rang with small-boy laughter and a hundred happy sounds of days gone by.

In the far niche of the court, Elimelech had always done his work, his foot pumping the treadle and the clay spinning softly, casting a spell of contented industry over his home.

Naomi's gaze settled there now, and her hands trembled.

"No," she said softly, "our first duty will be to set up my husband's potting wheel. We will clean out his favorite corner and establish his place before all others. It is only fitting."

CHAPTER SIX

As in any community dependent on the soil, days in
Bethlehem began early. Though the actual work of
harvesting barley, which ringed the town in outlying
fields, did not begin until late morning, folk completed their daily chores ahead of that activity.

Water was drawn at the central well, animals fed
and tended, families prepared for a long day by
shortly after dawn.

But village bustle did not disturb Naomi's quiet
neighborhood, until the barley workers trekked to
their labor. At that time they passed directly under
the shadow of her roof, along the road skirting the
town wall. By wagon, on donkey, and by foot they
journeyed to the fields which now lay cool with dew,
but would soon be baking under the season's sun.

Two hours before noon, harvest would commence
in earnest, for the moisture stored in the grain over-
night would have dissipated, leaving the stalks pliable
and easy to cut.

Having lived a full week in the new residence,
Ruth had grown accustomed to the singing of wagon
wheels as they passed beyond the wall. She had also
grown attached to the privacy and charm of the little
retreat.

Early on, she had asked Naomi how Elimelech had
fared so well at his business, tucked away in this

sleepy end of town. Mahlon and Chilion had plied their trade on the main thoroughfare of Kir-Hareseth, and had benefited by the exposure.

"My husband's work needed little publicity," the old woman explained. "He was an artist, not an entrepreneur. Folks from all Judea sought him out."

But Ruth wondered how far the long-lost husband's reputation would carry Naomi now. And this morning she feared for her own welfare as she prepared breakfast from the dwindling reserves of their larder.

Recently, several of Naomi's old friends had come by with loaves, cakes, and sacks of meal. Though neither Ruth nor the mother-in-law had breathed a word of their increasingly desperate state, it could not have escaped observant onlookers that matters were tight for the two women.

When everyone shopped in the same marketplace, and rubbed elbows over the same produce, folk could easily detect when a neighbor was in straits. Choicer cuts of meat were passed over in favor of less expensive pieces; well-formed fruit, in favor of the bruised and inferior.

This morning, Ruth dished out the last of the golden wheat brought from Moab and proceeded to prepare a light-textured bread, which might be their last such delicacy for some time. Inexpensive carp imported from the Lake of Chinnereth would provide their protein for the day.

As she formed the bread dough into a heavy ball, she studied her hands, still well cared for and youthful. And she remembered having noticed the hands of other women at market, those of the reaper, winnower, and gleaner classes who labored daily in the barley fields. Small red cuts and a rough, chapped appearance aged their hands before their time, and merely to look at them caused pain.

Barley must be terribly coarse stuff, Ruth surmised, itchy and miserable to work with.

As the last of the wheat flour was devoured into the moist dough, her heart sped anxiously. Barley cakes were the fare of poor people, and soon, it seemed, she and Naomi would be dining on the fibrous stuff.

Placing the substance into the clay oven, Ruth stood up and rubbed the small of her back. In a couple of hours the sun would be risen over the courtyard, and yet Naomi still had not stirred from her bedchamber. This tardiness was unlike the industrious woman, and only further evidence of her depressed spirit.

As Ruth went to the gallery to waken the matron, she glanced around the intimate patio. She was amazed at how quickly she had come to love this place, and realized that she felt closer to Mahlon in this corner of the world.

She had always known he longed for Bethlehem, but now she could appreciate his attachment more than ever—an attachment which, while rooted in the little abode of his birth, had grown to encompass the environs of Bethlehem, from streets and walls to rolling hills beyond. And she could imagine that when Elimelech was alive, before Naomi's heart had died with him, the family had been close indeed.

Stepping up to the widow's chamber, Ruth tapped lightly on the door. "Mother, breakfast will soon be ready," she called.

A faint rustling of bedclothes told her the old

woman was awake. But after waiting some moments without a reply, Ruth shrugged her shoulders and decided to go to the roof while the bread baked.

Below, on the highway, the last of the workers trekked to the fields. Their wagons and beasts were free of burden, but by evening would be laden with sheaves of grain, lashed to donkey backs and laid out beneath tarps on cart floors.

As Ruth peered into the wagons, she could see children playing hide-and-seek beneath the empty coverings, and her heart surged unexpectedly. This of all thoughts was her saddest, that she had never blessed Mahlon with a child—that there was no son to carry on his line.

She was past some of her grief. Of late she had not wept so often as she used to. But she was still vulnerable to sudden reminders of her loss.

Scenes from Mahlon's funeral flashed before her. And as if it had been yesterday, she could hear the rabbi's oration, delivered at the gravesite.

"Weep sore for him that goeth away," he had chanted the traditional eulogy, "for he shall return no more."

This statement was reserved, Ruth had been told, for those who died without progeny. For, when a man departed this life childless, the Jews maintained, it was as though he had never lived.

Never lived! Ruth's brow knitted in angry furrows. Such a belief was against nature—against life itself! Of all men, Mahlon *had* lived, his soul vibrant and generous. And all who knew him were better for having received of his spirit.

Nonetheless, she was saddened. How much kinder

death would have been, had only an heir been born to preserve her husband's name on the earth!

Setting her shoulders squarely, however, the Moabitess told herself that this time grief would not overcome her. She might never cease to mourn the death of Mahlon, but she would not let her soul wither as Naomi had. At that point, she would depart from her mother-in-law's way.

As she asserted this, her rooftop surveillance fell upon a spectacle of uncommon delight. A horseman passed upon the road, a strong and handsome man, whose manner and bearing arrested her attention on the instant.

His horse, alone, was a captivating sight, its pale, creamy coat a sheen beneath the morning sun, and its full white mane and tail draped magnificently against the Bethlehem breeze. But the rider was the greater attraction. Broad-shouldered, he carried his middle-aged body well, groomed not pristinely, but in keeping with his apparently noble class.

It was clear he was a person of distinction, for those he passed bowed their heads in respectful greeting. Though Ruth could not make out his words, he seemed to address each villager with kindness. And while he was garbed for a day in the fields, his habit was of fine material, rugged and simple, but worthy of him.

His tunic, which fell to calf-high sandal laces of well-worked leather, was nearly the same color as his horse, and contrasted pleasantly with his dark beard and hair.

Silver streaks at his temples told he was not a young man, and yet days in the outdoors had burnished his skin to complement the look of age, and his face was smooth in the sun. Something in his demeanor struck Ruth as familiar.

As she contemplated this, however, her focus was interrupted. Naomi had risen, at last, and sought her out.

"I smell the bread baking, my dear," she said. "You have been busy already."

"Yes." Ruth smiled, departing for the stairs. "I am glad you are up. I will put the fish on the fire."

When she had left, the matron went quickly to the rooftop rail and bent over it, hoping to see whom the girl studied so intently.

CHAPTER
SEVEN

The day before Sabbath was always a busy one in
Jewish communities. Marketplaces stayed open until
the very edge of sunset, when the traditional twenty-
four-hour rest began, and would not reopen until two
mornings later. Therefore all buying of goods to
carry families through the intervening holiday must
be completed before dark.

Bethlehem's pre-Sabbath bustle was typical. But
today, Ruth did not compete for the best wares on the
merchant benches, nor push quickly through the
press with arms full of produce. Instead she waited
until the crowd had diminished, and until the shopkeepers were ready to pack up their goods, before
she began to select her purchases.

By now, hawkers would be less apt to bargain, and
might take what they were offered, to dispense with
leftover inventory. And what was left over would be
the fare of poor folk who could not afford the best.

Ruth was poor. There was no denying it. The two
widows of Moab had come here barely more than
destitute, and with no prospects.

The young woman had not left Kir-Hareseth with
any illusions. But, now that she faced hunger, she
knew fear as she had never known it.

Ruth waited in the widening shadow of Bethlehem's
gate, as the last of the shoppers turned for home.

Then, with her mantle drawn far over her head, nearly concealing her face, she approached the first stall, where a pile of bruised apricots from Gilead had been left. Offering the merchant a pittance, she took what would have been destined for the garbage cart, and moved on to the baker's booth.

From counter to counter she proceeded, trying to satisfy her satchel with enough food for two days, and trying, at the same time, to ignore the shopkeepers' pitying glances, their awkward silences.

It did seem, as she had come to know the Judeans, that they were a kinder community than the Jews of Moab. Beyond some initial concern over Naomi's welfare being in the hands of this young foreigner, they had quickly accepted the girl, and had been more than civil with her.

Perhaps the strain of dealing with a pagan culture hardened those who lived outside Israel. Naomi would surely say so.

But, despite the kindness of folks here, today Ruth kept her face averted, avoiding their sympathetic gazes.

As she turned for home, calculating how best to make the small sack of supplies stretch through Sabbath, her attention was drawn to the gate where a large group of barley workers was just returning from the fields.

She had seen these folk before. They were not hired laborers—the reapers or winnowers. These were the gleaners, a poor class who were allowed by the Law of Moses to follow after the field hands, picking up whatever grain was left behind.

The laws of Israel were, in fact, quite liberal toward the distressed and even the foreigner who could not make a living in the land. In vineyards and olive plantations, fallen fruit was to be left for the widow, the orphan, and the dispossessed. The owner of a grain field was not to wholly reap the corners of his land, nor the extreme edge, and he was not to gather up the ears and heads remaining upon the ground once the reapers had passed over.

Since the Hebrews had learned agriculture during their four hundred years' enslavement in Egypt, they had combined the shepherding instinct with love of the soil. The Mosaic state had been founded on farming and everywhere throughout Judea grain fields and plantations dominated the scene, the herdsmen taking fields further from town.

Husbandry of any kind was held in high esteem. Almost every family had a stake in the land, and ownership could never be revoked. But the poor were not overlooked. And those who benefited from the soil were bound to share their profit with folk less fortunate.

Such were those who now sought the shelter of Bethlehem's walls or made their way toward the depressed section of town, where housefronts were shabby and children slept on dirty pallets.

They entered the gate beneath the gaze of city patriarchs who were, themselves, turning for home. These were the village leaders, to whom the affairs of justice and public issue were brought for counsel.

Ruth had noticed the elders often, most of them gray-haired, like the rabbi of Kir-Hareseth, and with long beards. The majority were venerable fellows, with kind eyes and wise faces. Among them, however, were a few whose austere bearing marked them with the rigidity and cold traditionalism reminiscent of Moab's Jewish master.

All day they had sat at the gate, the customary meeting place of Jewish town courts. Beneath their arms they carried thick rolls of parchment, bundled for the night in leather wrappers. Ruth knew these were copies of Jewish Law and Scripture, the oracles of the Israelites, which to her were still foreign.

She surveyed the group of holy men with private awe, her eyes lingering upon the scrolls as upon a great mystery.

But then she was struck by the expressions on some of the elders' faces. They watched the poor folk, with their armloads and satchels of gleaned barley, entering from the fields. Compassion was evident here and there, but a number betrayed cool condescension, and even haughty disdain.

Small children and old women were bid "good-day," but at the same time holy cloaks were drawn tight about unfeeling shoulders. And though the crippled and the bent were acknowledged with a nod, prideful eyes scorned them from behind as they passed.

Ruth gathered up her own meager gleanings, the battered market produce, and made her way toward home, ready to spend the weekend observing the Jewish Sabbath. But as she went she marveled at the conundrum of piety which she had just observed, and at the hypocrisy for which she had no explanation.

CHAPTER
EIGHT

The morning after Sabbath dawned bright over Naomi's court. Ruth paced the colored pavement of the patio nervously, as the first fingers of sunlight roused the sleeping town.

She had been awake most of the night, preparing to take up arms against her poverty. Memories of Kir-Hareseth and the luxuries of childhood had haunted her mercilessly through the dark hours. She questioned bitterly her decision in leaving Moab, as hunger pangs stabbed her ribs.

Naomi, it was clearer every day, had no strength to pursue a solution. Her initial drive to be home had dwindled the first day here, and despite the kindness of neighbors and relatives, had never revived.

This had baffled the daughter-in-law. But it occurred to Ruth, now, that Naomi had not really returned to Israel to renew her life or to find joy. She had returned home . . . to die!

Perhaps the matron could not have admitted this to anyone before she left Moab. Perhaps she had not even known it herself.

But it was more evident every morning that the woman was foundering, that if something did not change soon, she would succumb mortally to the wounds of her past.

It would not be advanced age or ill health which

would kill Naomi. After all, she was not *that* old. And though her sons had been frail in youth and her husband had died prematurely, her body had always been strong.

No — it was hopelessness and a life of disappointed dreams which had incapacitated her. And no longer did she repeat her prayers or sing her psalms on the rooftop; no longer did she lift her eyes skyward.

Presently, however, Ruth cared for more than Naomi's decline. In the night she had come to grips with the harsh reality that life for both of them, not only emotionally, but physically, was sorely threatened. And she knew her own energy must be turned to the task of survival, whether or not the elder ever rallied.

As Ruth waited for her mother-in-law to waken, she smoothed the bodice of her simple homespun tunic, the only one of its kind that her father had ever made her. She used to wear it when she helped her mother with the heaviest cleaning chores, and when Naomi assigned her the most rigorous tasks at Elimelech's house. Today she wore it to enlist in labor to which she was unaccustomed, the thought of which wearied her already.

She folded and refolded the burlap bag used for Sabbath groceries, and anxiously stuffed it under her arm, hoping it would be full by day's end.

Meanwhile, she glanced repeatedly at the gallery, wishing to see Naomi — before traffic beyond the wall signaled the hour to depart. As morning advanced, she grew more careful of the time, and at last went to rouse her mother-in-law.

Stepping into the chamber, its light muted by heavy window tapestries, she tiptoed up to the woman's pallet, and bent over her.

"Mother," she whispered.

Naomi's eyelids fluttered, and she sat up with a start, thinking for the instant that Ruth was some phantom. A quick groan escaped her, as the girl touched her gently on the shoulder.

"Elimelech . . . " The word rattled past dry lips.

"No, Mother," the visitor whispered, sitting down beside her. "It is I, Ruth. I must speak with you."

Naomi drew away, her brow furrowed. "Are you all right, child?" she asked. "What hour is it?"

"It is early morning. And I am well. I must speak with you."

The matron pulled a light shawl over her shoulders and tried to adjust her eyes to the dimness, as Ruth raced through her little speech.

"There is only a small bit of food in our larder," she reminded her. "We have no prospects, and our money is nearly gone. Friday, at market, I once again saw the workers returning from the fields."

Naomi listened carefully, trying to anticipate her point.

"I am going today to join the laborers in the harvest," Ruth announced.

The elder bore a blank expression. "You have no training for winnowing," she objected, "and reaping is mainly man's work. What are you thinking?"

"Mother," Ruth said firmly, "you know what I intend to do. The gleaners. . . . "

But Naomi shook her head. "No!" she asserted.

"Never has the family of Elimelech taken to scavenging!"

Ruth was incredulous. "Never has the family of Elimelech taken to starving, either!" she argued. "Do you have another suggestion?"

The widow was taken aback, and a twitch worked at her mouth. "Why, yes," she stammered. "We have only been here two weeks. I fully intend to set up some sort of business. And the vacant field left by my husband . . . I plan to sell it."

The Moabitess looked deep into the old woman's eyes, realizing as never before the extent of her detachment from reality. A new occupation at Naomi's age was out of the question, and it could take months to sell a piece of unplanted property.

"Proceed as you will," Ruth said kindly. "But meanwhile, something must be done to carry us through."

Then, rising from the pallet, she secured the burlap bag once more beneath her arm and studied the Jewess's furtive face. With all the respect she could muster, she deferred to the matron's authority.

"I ask permission, Mother," she said. "But I *will* do what must be done. Please let me go to the field and glean among the ears of grain after one in whose sight I may find favor."

Naomi studied her companion's solid stance, and at last looked at the floor. "You know it can be dangerous in a man's world," she warned. "Things do not always go well for young women."

"I know," the girl conceded. "Do I have your permission?"

"Go, my daughter," Naomi said with a sigh.

And as Ruth exited, the old woman lay back on her pillow, glad for the first time that her husband was not here—that he was spared the sight of her destitution.

CHAPTER
NINE

Ruth waited at the small back gate of Bethlehem, closest to Naomi's house, and watched the midmorning traffic. Her heart pushed against her chest in an anxious rhythm. She must fall in with the poor folk who would soon be taking up the rear of the parade making its way to the barley fields.

The prospect was frightening for many reasons. To begin with, she was alone. No one came to help her break her way into the company of strangers. Also, she was a woman, and always—in all places, at all times—as Naomi had indicated, it was dangerous for a female to venture unescorted into unfamiliar territory. Finally, she was a foreigner, and this above all would set her in a hard place. For there was just enough difference in her speech and manner to mark her as an alien. Therefore, despite the warm reception of Naomi's friends in town, she would be vulnerable to social prejudice when away from that connection.

Most demoralizing, however, was the reality that her station in life had come to this—that she, a privileged daughter of Moab, should find herself forced to mingle with the destitute and helpless of the earth.

But she could linger no longer in the shade of Bethlehem's wall. Taking a deep breath, she drew her mantle over her head, half covering her face, and prepared to step into the file of oncoming gleaners. Holding her bag in tight fingers, with her arms crossed over her stomach, she waited for a convenient opening and sidled into the shuffle.

The fine dust which had settled over the road, blown in from harvested fields, was raised in a perpetual billow by the trampling line ahead, and quickly climbed upward, clinging to her tunic. Soon, she knew, she would *look* like a gleaner, an unwashed and unkempt follower of the more privileged laborers. Before she ever arrived at work, she would bear the mark of poverty.

Anxiety had almost replaced the ache of hunger. But the long trek toward the fields resurrected it.

She could not appreciate the beauty of the terrain, the golden sea crisscrossed by shining canals, by evenly measured hedges and low stone walls. Immaculate terraces robed sloping hills, delineating garden spots and plantations, as well as "resting" acres, from those currently in use. For Jehovah gave all things a Sabbath in Israel, including the land, and each field had its years of quiet fallow.

Early in the season the earth had been cleared of stones and rubble. And no decent farmer would sow among thorns, lest his reputation as well as his work be sorely threatened. Therefore each parcel was pristinely manicured, all new land plowed twice, hoed, and harrowed to a powder, until not a clod remained.

The seed, sometimes sown and harrowed at the same time, was often plowed in with a cross furrow, and the grain stood in even, predictable rows. For it was a matter of pride in Israel that one's fields be orderly, as the Law of God is orderly.

But such matters were immaterial to Ruth. If she was aware of anything in the setting along the road, it was the odor of salted compost, and the black of burned-over stubble.

For all the land, this time of year, smelled of death as well as new life. Straw-trodden dung and animal carcasses, with their blood, had been used throughout fall and winter to fertilize the ground. And the lingering odor of decay mingled with the charred remains of noxious herbs and weeds, in testimony to nature's enforced balance.

As Ruth walked, she reached into her bag, the small one suspended from her belt, and drew out a chunk of bread. She had not yet eaten anything today, knowing that the loaf she brought must stretch until she returned home.

She could not give thanks as she contemplated the crude fare. This was a barley cake, hard evidence of her low condition—the food of beasts, the manna of oxen and asses.

Noting the near-empty purses of her fellow gleaners, however, she knew she was not alone in her extremity, and so she devoured the meal humbly.

Once the gnawing hunger had been quieted, Ruth was able to focus on the poor folk with whom she traveled. They were of all ages and they seemed to represent a variety of nationalities, though she could not precisely label their origins. Most of them were elderly and many, besides herself, were female—probably widows who had no means of livelihood other than itinerant field work.

What struck her most deeply, however, were the

children—gaunt, dirty, shabbily garbed. For an instant, she was actually glad she had never borne Mahlon an heir. For what conditions would such a child have inherited? And she was happy that no one but herself and Naomi suffered the hunger and despair which resulted from their own choice.

Ahead, among the reapers and winnowers, was the buzz of friendly conversation. Some even chanted lively songs, approaching their day with delight.

"Labor is a blessing," the Jews taught. "All work is really for God." While the philosophers of other nations saw toil as a curse, incompatible with the privileges of citizenship, pride in labor among the Jews could be quite an affectation at times. Ruth recalled Mahlon's quoting of an admonition: "Fair is the study of the Law, if accompanied by worldly occupation. To engage in both is to keep away sin."

But at the rear of the marching throng, among the gleaners, there was no such attitude, no such song, and no encouraging chatter. In fact, most of these folk guarded the path beneath their feet territorially, saying little.

For this, also, Ruth was grateful. She did not care to exchange words with anyone.

The barley fields were on every side, now. Already the string of gleaners was splitting off, heading in different directions for acres which had not been reaped.

There was a definite sense of competition between them. Ruth stood still in the middle of the road, watching the more experienced itinerants as they hurried for the choicest plots, behind the field hands.

Most of them, it appeared, were familiar to the

reapers. They required no permission to fall in behind the crews. But no one knew Ruth, and she wondered just how to go about gaining access.

Perhaps if she simply applied to the nearest family, she could study their labor and follow in kind.

She watched a bent matron and her half-dozen grandchildren as they scurried to the border of a field now being harvested, and she traced their steps at a cautious distance. When the reapers had scythed an ample swath, leaving one corner uncut, she waited until the old woman had begun to strip it. The children were intent on their part of the work, pulling handfuls of standing grain out by the roots and laying them in bundles on the grandmother's open arms, when Ruth came upon them.

She began her own gleaning by gathering small piles of missed barley, not intruding on the richer cache which the family had claimed. But almost the instant she touched the field, six pair of young eyes, and one old pair, snapping and flashing, fell upon her.

"You're not welcome here!" the grandmother declared. "Find yourself another place."

Ruth, chagrined, took her empty satchel and retreated, her face red and tears nudging at her eyes. But the woman shouted after her angrily, "Next time, get clearance by the manager!"

Making her way to the road, she stood once more in the center and surveyed the bustling workers scattered all around. How was she to know one man from another? Would a "manager" bear an insignia, or be garbed distinctively?

Following the highway a great distance, she at last

came to a portion of the field which seemed to be populated by fewer gleaners, perhaps because it lay so far from town. And it struck her as intriguing that the poor folk who did trail the reapers through this parcel did not confine themselves to the edges of the plot, but worked directly beside the hired hands among the sheaves themselves. Thus they were allowed to pick up the choicest leavings as the barley was bundled.

Furthermore, she noted that several of the reapers were young women, suntanned and robust, apparently maidservants of the landowner. While harvesting was generally a male profession, the employer of this crew seemed to see merit in the work of females, and from this Ruth took courage.

She had often heard tales of the dangers of venturing into the world of manly labor. In Moab it was emphasized from a girl's earliest years that she was better off to stay close to home. And from what little Ruth had learned of Moses' laws, Israel was not unfamiliar with such matters.

Specific injunctions had been established with reference to the personal safety of females who found it necessary to leave the city for work on the land. But the necessity of such laws only served to illustrate just how far from Jehovah's heart the people could wander.

Therefore, it was comforting to see that in this field, at least, many young women worked side by side. There was safety in numbers. And Ruth longed to attach herself to this plot.

Taking a deep breath, she set foot on the acreage, and walked cautiously toward one of the hands, whose gray hair indicated he might be in charge. He was bent over a bundle of grain, securing it in a sheaf, as Ruth stepped behind him.

"Sir," she whispered, clearing her throat.

He paid no heed, apparently not hearing her, and so she repeated herself.

The worker stood up in surprise, wiping his hands on his cloak and eyeing her with care. Again, he said nothing, and so she continued, her pulse racing.

"Sir, I wish to join your harvest," she petitioned.

The laborer wiped his perspiring brow and snorted impatiently. "We have enough reapers," he objected, "and plenty of winnowers. Try again at fall harvest."

Ruth fumbled with her satchel. "No, sir, I spoke amiss," she stammered. "I do not wish to be hired. I . . . I wish to glean."

At this the reaper lifted his chin, surveying her up and down. With a shrug, he grumbled, "You'll have to talk to the manager."

"Oh," Ruth replied. "I assumed you must be he."

The elderly fellow was taken aback, and not a little flattered. Suddenly his demeanor softened and he seemed to pay her more mind. "Why, miss, I thank you," he said smiling, "but I shall never have such rank, if I live to be a hundred. But, here," he offered, holding out his hand. "I can show you the way."

Hesitantly, Ruth took his arm as he led her across the field toward a large portable awning, erected as a shelter against the sun, under which field hands took their breaks. "The foreman usually abides here during the mornings," he explained, "working on his accounts."

The reaper's voice had picked up spirit as he escorted her toward the tent, and she could not help but notice a certain lively pride in his step as he ushered her past his fellow workers.

Young men and old, alike, stood up to watch as the fair Moabitess was led before them, and Ruth's cheeks burned as they scrutinized her, leaning together for appreciative whispers or leering grins.

Anxiously she surveyed the fields for the young ladies whose very presence had given her courage to advance. But by now they had worked far out into the parcel, and though grouped together, could not be supportive at this distance.

She was a woman alone in a male world. And never had she felt so alien. While all eyes were on her, many were wanton eyes, and while tongues discussed her, it was not necessarily with empathy.

At last the tent was within reach, and as the old reaper led her to it, he bowed low, leaving her to await the manager's attention.

The foreman, who sat at a small table, a pile of parchment before him on which were arrayed columns of figures, did not glance up for some time. And when he did finally acknowledge Ruth's presence, he still had not looked upon her.

"What is it?" he muttered, assuming some employee needed assistance.

Again she addressed a stranger. "Sir, I ask permission to glean in your field."

The manager, hearing the female voice, focused on her briefly, and then more carefully. Despite her simple attire, and the road dust which clung to her face, she was a thing of beauty. On the instant his mind registered trouble. Studying her dark, braided tresses where they peeked from beneath her veil, and the liquid green of her eyes, he shook his head.

Again a blush rose to Ruth's olive cheeks, and she glanced at the ground. But this further troubled the man, who sensed her innocent nature.

"Women must be strong to work here," he growled, trying to sound firm.

"I am strong," Ruth answered quickly. "I have traveled far and I work hard for my mother-in-law."

The manager sighed. "I do not speak of physical strength alone, my lady," he explained, "though that, too, is important. No—you must be strong of character."

Ruth interpreted his meaning, and anger pricked her. "What do you take me for?" she asked. "I am not a. . . ."

"Oh, dear girl," he laughed, "I do not question your integrity. I only mean that things do not always go . . . easily . . . for women in the fields."

Though hardened by years of overseeing rowdy hands, the manager was awkward with the subject.

"I understand." Ruth nodded. "Now, sir, may I glean here?"

The fellow sensed her strength of will.

"Days are hot . . . hours long . . . , " he warned.

"Sir," she repeated, "may I?"

With a shrug, the foreman nodded. "You may," he at last allowed.

Ruth bowed gratefully, and began to back away. As she stood to go, however, she surveyed the field again, and thought to pursue his kindness further. "Please," she added, "let me glean and gather after the reapers . . . among the sheaves."

The employer was confounded by her courage, and asked in amazement, "Where do you hail from, and whose daughter-in-law are you?"

"I belong to Naomi Ben Elimelech, of Moab," she replied, "and have left my country to follow after her. My name is Ruth, widow of Mahlon."

Then studying him intently, she testified, "I am a daughter of Jehovah, though a stranger. And I will observe the ways of Israel in the fields."

The manager nodded. "I have heard good reports of the young lady who brought Naomi from that distant land. May God be with you."

And watching until she grew tense beneath his gaze, he considered all her request, and gave her leave to do as she pleased.

CHAPTER
TEN

The maidservants of this field were highly adept at their labor, and Ruth, being a novice at the art of gleaning, was hard pressed to keep up with them. As they went ahead, reaping and tying the grain into bundles, they took little heed of her, and often managed to collect the richest leavings before Ruth could reach them.

Though many of them recognized her as the one who had come with Naomi to Bethlehem, they did not engage her in conversation, and in fact generally bore themselves aloof from her.

Ruth, who had always been surrounded by female friends in Kir-Hareseth, sensed the snubbing keenly, but tried to concentrate on the work at hand. Occasionally, however, she did catch snatches of their gossip, which centered on the young fellows who worked the field all about, and on some mysterious man named "Boaz."

Their typically girlish chatter was sprinkled liberally with references to him, and when his name was mentioned, it was followed by giggles and sighs, indicative of the prominent role he played in their fantasies.

She could not help but wonder which of the many hands he might be. And occasionally, as she stood up to rest, she would survey the young bucks here and there, trying to imagine which deserved such applause.

But Ruth was not comfortable with such analysis. Not since she had married Mahlon had she contemplated other men, and she was not yet ready to do so.

The thought of romantic love was foreign to her now. She considered herself only a widow, nothing more. The hope of warm embraces and tender smiles had faded forever when Mahlon had died. And Naomi had become the young girl's world.

Rightfully so, she would have reasoned, had anyone challenged her. Who was she, that love should come her way again? When she compared herself, even fleetingly, to the healthy, apple-cheeked damsels who sang ahead of her, she withered inside.

A widow was one for whom the prospect of life must be eternally selfless, she imagined. Especially when one had no child, a career of sacrificial service was in order. She might cease, eventually, to grieve her losses, but she would never experience the joys of fleshly fulfillment again.

As for the male interest she had roused upon entering the field today, she passed it off as pure wolfishness, and could not envision any man developing sincere concern for her again.

As her mind wandered over these things, she was unaware that the lively girls worked their way far ahead of her. As she stuffed small handfuls of chaffy stalks into her satchel, the gap between herself and the sheave-maidens was widening.

There were no singing birds to be silenced, and few humming insects during the heat of day to stop their chorus. But the presence of nearing danger was signaled by something intangible, by a sudden racing of Ruth's pulse, and by an unaccountable stillness in the air.

Looking discreetly ahead, she found that she was indeed alone in the field, and then peering carefully over her shoulder, she saw that she would not long be.

She did not know his name, nor did he introduce himself. He only told her his intentions by a loosening of his belt as he approached, and by his deceptively soothing tone.

"You are Mahlon's widow?" he inquired. "Then you are not a virgin, and no one will have to know."

Ruth's face was covered with a veil to keep dangerous chaff from invading her lungs. And yet the stranger seemed to strip it with a look, and to disrobe her entirely with his eyes.

"Sir, I will not join you," she said weakly, her head swimming with fear.

"But, you have no choice," he laughed. "We are alone."

A pile of sheaves lay a few feet away, and as he glanced at it now, she knew his plans.

He drew near slowly, his brown face crinkled in smile lines, but there was no love in his heart.

"How do you know me?" she cried.

"I was in the crowd the day you came to Bethlehem."

Ruth did not recall seeing him, having focused on no one but Abigail that weary evening.

"Did you know my husband?" she asked, frantically trying to challenge him.

"I did, when we were boys," he replied absently, taking her by the arm.

"Then, sir, how can you think to sin against his memory?"

The assailant was not listening. His eyes were on the sheave-pile and he rudely turned her in that direction.

Now her heart pounded like a drum, and she peered wildly about for help. No one was near, and she feared to cry aloud.

Still, she must not let this happen. "Lord Jehovah!" she screamed as he thrust her to the ground behind the concealing sheaves, tearing her outer garment and removing his cloak.

As the shadow of his naked body fell upon her, his two hands clutching the earth on either side, and his breath hot upon her neck, she grabbed a fistful of fibrous slivers left from the bundled grain. Raising it to his face, she smeared it into his open eyes and watched as he reared back, afire with excruciating pain.

Scooting out from beneath him, Ruth stood up and ran across the field. The manager's tent seemed years away, but she would reach it, though the ground itself arose to hold her back.

CHAPTER
ELEVEN

Tears stung Ruth's dark lashes as she sat, trembling, in the shade of the manager's awning. Not only was she terrified by the attack of the would-be rapist, but she sensed that the foreman was less than sympathetic.

Of course, she could have expected as much. She was a newcomer, having just this morning begged his indulgence; and she was a Moabitess, a foreigner—a poor one, at that. Though he had claimed knowledge of her kindness to Naomi, surely he viewed her now as nothing more than an itinerant troublemaker. After all, had he not warned her to watch out for just such dangers in the field?

Perhaps he did not even believe her story. Perhaps he wondered if his warning had gone to her head and she had simply mistaken some field hand's innocent flirtation.

But Ruth knew the truth of the matter. The image of the assailant's face and the smell of his breath would never leave her. She would have simply deserted this place seeking another employer, had the manager not insisted she stay until the owner of the field arrived.

"Send for Ben Salmon," he had growled to one of the servants. "He will want to question the girl."

He may as well have said "inquisition," so biting

was the word. Whoever the landlord was—this Ben Salmon—he surely would have no compassion.

Ruth studied her hands, already chapped by the brief work time she had put in. They lay in small knots upon her lap, an indistinct blur through her tears.

Her right fist clenched repeatedly, as though reliving the act which had driven her pursuer away—and had her eyes been able to focus, she would have seen that pieces of chaff were still embedded in her fingertips. What she could not have perceived were the scrapings of his skin which clung beneath her nails. But his memory was clear enough.

Suddenly, Ruth longed to be home, to bury her head on Naomi's shoulder and draw some comfort from her.

Men of the fields came and went, drinking from the water jugs beneath the awning, or convening with the manager over business. If they noticed Ruth, the foreman replied to their quizzical looks in a whisper.

Most of them laughed. A few did not.

But none of them was Ben Salmon.

Morning passed, and time for the midday meal would soon be upon them. Ruth, having eaten nothing since dawn but one crude barley loaf, was famished. She held her stomach tightly, sweltering in the heat which permeated the tent's dark interior, and listening to the rhythm of distant scythes until she grew faint.

Presently, however, the incessant drone of harvest was broken by the stamp of a horse's hooves outside the canopy.

The angle of the awning cut off from her view all

but the creature's legs and the tip of its bannerlike tail. But it must be a horse of great importance, for the instant the manager heard its step, he was on his feet and outside the tent to greet the rider.

"May the Lord be with you," she heard the newcomer call.

"May the Lord bless you," many voices returned, those in the field and nearby as well.

This must be Ben Salmon! Ruth sighed deeply and tried to compose herself for the coming interview. She did not have long to wait, for now he was inside the tent, followed close behind by the foreman.

It was clear the owner had been summoned from a hard morning's work, for his clothes were dusty as a field hand's after riding through many acres and overseeing his employees. As his eyes adjusted to the dim light of the awning, he seemed not to see Ruth, who sat in the darkest corner. He only sat quickly on a stool and began to unlace his sandals.

The manager knelt immediately before him, placing a bowl of cool water on the ground and commencing to wash his feet.

Ruth was glad that the wealthy man had not focused on her, for though he would not have known her, she instantly recognized him. He was the handsome horseman who had passed beneath her gaze as she had watched from Naomi's balustrade.

When Ben Salmon raised a damp cloth to his perspiring forehead, and ran it over his face, Ruth's heart raced again, not this time for fear, but in response to the picture of him. He was, indeed, a handsome man—rugged and ruddy—his skin golden in the lamplight which reflected off the manager's table.

When she had seen him upon the highway, he had seemed familiar to her, but she could not tell why. Now she was struck by the same intuition, but once more had no explanation for it.

In some ways he reminded her of Mahlon—a little older, and of a more robust build—but bearing a kinship with him in brow and chin.

As she considered this, the fear of his coming questions rose afresh. She wished for him to think well of her, and to have no misconceptions regarding her character. Suddenly this was very important.

But she had no time to formulate her defense. For just as Ben Salmon set aside his towel, his eyes fell upon her.

"Whose young woman is this?" he asked, his voice bearing more than cursory interest.

She felt the familiar blush rise to her face, as the manager explained. "This is the lady who brought complaint, Master. The Moabitess, Ruth, who returned with Naomi Ben Elimelech from the country of Moab."

The landowner leaned forward from his stool, his hands upon his spread knees, studying her intently. Ruth could not interpret his look—whether it was of compassion or of doubt.

The manager, realizing that he could be taken to task for introducing a troublemaker to the field, continued to explain his decision with nervous speed. " 'Please let me glean and gather,' she said, 'even among the sheaves,' " he added, shrugging as if her very request had overwhelmed him. "Thus she came," he went on, implying that he had had little to say about her being in his employ. "And she has remained from morning until now."

Ben Salmon listened respectfully, but perhaps saw deeper than the manager's words. For when the foreman leaned close, whispering privately, "She has been sitting in the tent for a little while," the master rebuked him soundly.

"A little while? The poor girl is baking as though in an oven!" he growled. "How long have you kept her here?"

The manager shuffled uneasily. "Why, since she brought me her story—"

"That would be two hours ago!" Ben Salmon interrupted. "And you have done nothing to comfort her?"

"Well—she has been resting—"

"She has been your prisoner!" the owner snapped. "Am I to conclude that you did not believe her report?"

"Master, you know how it is with foreigners. . . . "

At this Ben Salmon stood and turned his back to his servant, making it clear he wished to hear no more. He drew near to Ruth, asking her to step into the light.

She did so and he pulled up the stool on which he had been sitting, offering it to her. When she had seated herself again he studied her hot face and trembling hands.

"Her cloak is torn, and there are scrapes upon her legs. See here," he said to the foreman, asking her to lift her garment a bit, so that the evidence of her struggle might be seen.

"Field work is hard," Ben Salmon said, "but she

could scarcely have suffered this damage in the short time she spent gleaning."

His voice was insistent, his face stern as he thus rebuked the manager. "Tell me," he demanded, "on what basis could you deny that something terrified this girl?"

"Sir . . . , " the foreman began weakly.

But Ben Salmon had no use for him. "Leave us!" he ordered. "I will speak with her in private."

The foreman bowed tensely and exited, leaving the landlord and his gleaner to themselves.

Ruth marveled at the turn of events, and wondered why this wealthy Israelite had taken so kindly to her.

But he was speaking again now, actually kneeling before her apologetically.

"I am Boaz Ben Salmon," he introduced himself, "and I beg your pardon for the hard thing you endured in my field."

The Moabitess could not hide her surprise. So this—this prince on the creamy stallion—was *the* Boaz whom the maidens had praised in the harvest. Of course, they were right. Who in Israel could compare with this gentleman?

Ruth, however, was speechless.

The wealthy Jew, concerned at her silence, tried to draw her out. "My lady," he began, "can you describe your attacker? Do you know his identity?"

The girl sighed, looking at the floor. Tears rose to her eyes as she explained, "I shall never forget him, my lord. But any description I could give would fit a thousand men. In his appearance, there was nothing unusual."

Boaz could believe this. Especially at this season,

when the field hands were all dusty and unkempt, dressed much alike, such anonymity was credible.

"There was one thing, however," she added, and Ben Salmon took heed. "He said he had known my husband. Perhaps they were once playmates."

Boaz ran this through his mind, but shrugged. "Again," he replied, "such a thing could be said for many men in the village."

Ruth was downcast, and the landlord, sensing her disappointment, tried to turn her thoughts to other things. "Tell me," he said, "why did you choose to glean—and why did you select my parcel for your labors?"

The Moabitess thrilled to the tenderness of his voice, and did not know what to make of it. But considering that he probably would have treated any distressed female with such compassion, she tried to contain her racing fantasies.

"Sir, my mother-in-law and I had little when we left my country. I had no choice but to follow after this work." She took a deep breath and tried not to look too plainly into his dark eyes. "Your harvest seemed open to women—something which I found encouraging. And I saw the liberality with which the gleaners were allowed to go among the sheaves."

Boaz smiled warmly. "Surely you will not fear to enter my field again. I cannot deny that such abuses as you have endured are common in Israel. And for this I humbly apologize. That a fine lady should venture into Judea in good faith, only to be so used, is a criminal thing. But I vow to you," he swore, "that should I ever discover who mistreated you, he *shall* be punished!"

Ruth studied her companion with round eyes. "Sir—I would not expect you to do me such service. I shall simply apply for work in some other place."

The master would not hear of this, however. Imploring her, he said, "Listen carefully, my daughter. Do not go to glean in another field. Furthermore, do not leave this one, but stay here with my maids. Let your eyes be on the parcel which they reap, and follow after them, keeping very close. Indeed, I have already, on my way here, commanded the field hands not to touch you. When you are thirsty, go to the water jars and drink from what the servants draw."

The girl, who had suffered much in her choice to leave Chemosh, had never expected such kindness in her new homeland. Overcome with his magnanimity, she shook her head and tried to suppress her tears.

Sliding down from the stool, she knelt beside him and bowed herself to the ground.

"Why have I found favor in your sight, that you should take notice of me," she asked brokenly, "since I am but a foreigner?"

Boaz reached out and lifted her tear-streaked face. Plumbing the depths of her soul with his gaze, he explained. "All that you have done for your mother-in-law after the death of your husband has been fully reported to me, and how you left your father and your mother and the land of your birth, and came to a people that you did not previously know." Then, raising one finger and wiping away a trickle of her sorrow, he said, "May the Lord reward your work, and may your wages be full from the Lord, the God of Israel, under whose wings you have come to seek refuge."

CHAPTER
TWELVE

When Ruth left the tent, there was not much time remaining before the midday meal. The hottest hours would follow that, and therefore the afternoon break was incumbent upon all who worked the harvest.

Since Ruth had accomplished very little before the assailant interrupted her labors, she concentrated intently on the task at hand, hoping to fill her satchel at least once before the mandatory rest and the onset of the most torrid period.

While she managed to keep up with the servant girls this time, her heart was still in the tent with Boaz. When she was not attuned fearfully to every sound of masculine laughter in the fields, or to each noise of crackling twigs behind her, she was thinking of the master.

She tried to discount his attention. Surely he would have been so kind to any troubled soul.

Still, having come through many months of loneliness, wanting the warmth of male companionship but never dreaming it could be hers, she was vulnerable to the least tenderness. Of this, she was aware. And therefore, all the more, she tried to keep a reasonable perspective on the morning's events.

And was she not a recent widow? What right did she have to think on anyone but her departed husband?

Repeatedly she attempted to get a grip on her racing thoughts. But it was no use. Over and over the image of the nobleman and the sound of his voice replayed themselves in her mind.

"I am a youngster!" she chided herself. "No more mature than the silly girls who lisp and giggle about the man!"

No amount of self-castigation served to drive him from her consciousness, however. He seemed to have permanently affixed himself there.

Ruth's satchel was becoming very heavy, and her sore hands rebelled at the chore of dragging it any further. Raising it to her shoulders, she made her way to the gleaners' pile, along the edge of the field, and chose a bare spot on which to empty the contents. Depositing the stalks, she took off her mantle and covered the little mound, thus marking it as her own.

She was not displeased with her work, though it did not compare with the caches of more experienced itinerants. And she must collect a good deal more in order to have anything worth taking home.

Time had raced ahead of her all day, and as she stood up from her pile, she saw that the reapers were making their way toward the tent for lunch.

She had drained the last drop of sun-warmed water from her hip-flask, but was hesitant to take advantage of Boaz's offer that she drink from the cool jugs beside the awning. And she would never admit to anyone that she had no more food with her. She would simply blend into one of the small crowds of gleaners who were going to eat in the shadows cast by the sheave mountains, and there wait for mealtime to pass.

She was light-headed with hunger and thirst, however, and as she watched the workers disperse to the shady spots, she cursed herself for ever having left Moab.

As she stood paralyzed at the edge of the field, a voice drew her back to the moment. "Join me, my lady," it invited.

Boaz stood beside her, having come upon her on his way to join the workers at dinner. "You need not eat in the field," he said. "Bring your lunch and dine with me."

Ruth was, again, confounded by his generosity. But, at the same time, her cheeks reddened with shame.

"What is it?" he asked, contemplating her expression.

"I will stay with the gleaners," she hedged.

Boaz looked at the purse which hung empty on her belt, and asked her pointedly, "My lady, have you nothing to eat?"

Ruth fought tears once more, but at last sighed, "Nothing, my lord."

The master took her gently by the elbow. "Come here," he insisted. "You may eat of the common loaf at the reapers' tent and dip your bread in the wine."

There was no arguing with the man as he led her to the awning and sat her down in a cool spot beside the reapers themselves. All eyes were on her, the young maidens wondering at the meaning of Boaz's action, and the young men not wondering at all.

Quickly the master found a skin of "chomets," or sour wine, and poured an ample amount into a stoneware cup. Though it was a nonintoxicating beverage, the drink mainly of the poor, it was highly popular among Israel's manual laborers, for it was exhilarating and took well to the bread dipped in it. Ruth sipped the turbid liquid gingerly, uncertain of the aroma. And when her lips involuntarily puckered, the observant crew laughed heartily.

She was not offended, sensing their sudden acceptance of her. After all, it was clear she was the landlord's guest, and must be treated well.

Though it was a scorching afternoon, there was a small fire in the center of the tent, well away from the grain fields. The workers avoided it except to prepare another favorite staple—"parched corn," or roasted grain. This was *the* delicacy of harvest, enjoyed by all who were privileged to labor. When Boaz had brought Ruth the drink, he retired to the tent, where he set about to prepare her a small feast of the stuff.

She watched in humble amazement as he tied swatches of unripe stalks together in hand-sized bundles, and held the green ears above the flames. No one need tell her that this was beneath his station as a landowner. No one need tell her that Boaz was gracing her with extraordinary favor.

She studied him in silence, the too-familiar redness rising again to her cheeks. And as he sat beneath the dark canopy, leaning into the circle of firelight, she suddenly knew where she had first encountered him.

The figure who had walked at midnight upon the distant hillside balcony—the stranger who had captured her interest her first sleepless night in Bethlehem. This was Boaz!

As the gentle man left the tent, bringing to her a

plateful of roasted nuggets, she took it with trembling hands.

She longed to know him well, to understand his solitary way. For she perceived him to be a man apart, unlike any other in Israel.

But as mealtime passed, she was silent, realizing it was not her place to converse.

And when she rose at meal's end, bowing respectfully to him and departing for the field, she heard him speak to his servants in a firm whisper: "Let her glean, even among the sheaves. And do not insult her. And also, you shall purposely pull out for her some grain from the bundles and leave it, that she may collect it. And do not rebuke her."

CHAPTER
THIRTEEN

It was very late when Ruth entered the Bethlehem gate with a lively step. Though she was returning from a day of back-breaking labor, and though her fingers throbbed where small blade-fine cuts riddled them, she wore an infectious smile.

Upon her head, balanced by one hand, was her satchel, stuffed to the seams with an ephah of barley.

She would never forget the looks on the faces of her fellow gleaners when they, having beat out all the grain from their own collection of stalks, stood by watching Ruth's supply grow to at least twice the amount of the most experienced workers. Following their example, she had proceeded with the task of "rude threshing" doubtfully. After observing how it was done, she took a small stick and pounded the stalks to loosen the heads, then sorted out the largest hunks of chaff.

The other gleaners, not having been present at the lunch tent, did not know that Ruth's unusual luck that first day was the special providence of Boaz. They only stood by awestruck, imagining she must have learned a great deal of the art in Moab. That she looked nothing like a hardened itinerant and that her hands were obviously not work-callused, they accounted strange indeed. But weights and measures did not lie, and it was unquestioned that she had taken the championship for that day's earnings.

Surely Naomi will be proud! she thought as she rounded the last dark corner leading home.

When she stepped through the door, she found her mother-in-law waiting up, anxious for her return. And when Naomi saw the nearly bursting grain sack, she was incredulous.

Ruth lowered the heavy bag to the pavement and stood beside it proudly. "My daughter," the matron gasped, running her wizened hands over the surface of the plump, hard pillow, "how did you come by all this?"

"Run, Mother!" Ruth commanded. "Get the barrels and we will fill them."

Naomi quickly did as she was bid, bringing two wooden crocks to the fountain. Together the women divided the grain, Ruth marking one barrel for herself and one for the elder.

"There!" she cried. "We shall both be satisfied."

The mother-in-law burned with curiosity. "My daughter," she said again, "where did you glean today, and where did you work? May he who took notice of you be blessed!"

Ruth tried to temper her enthusiasm for the subject, knowing that Mahlon's mother would not appreciate her newborn feelings for the provider. "The name of the man with whom I worked today is Boaz," she replied, as matter-of-factly as possible.

To the girl's surprise, Naomi clasped her old hands before her, drawing them to her breast. Then with a sigh, eyes lifted heavenward, she cried, "May he be blessed of the Lord who has not withdrawn his kindness to the living and to the dead!" And then, grasping Ruth's two hands in her own, she exclaimed, "The man, Boaz, is our relative . . . one of our *closest* relatives!"

The gleaner's smile mellowed to a flicker at this news. So that was it! Ben Salmon had treated her well because he was a kinsman. How could she have been so foolish as to imagine he could care for her alone?

Wiping her hands upon her skirt, she drew the mortar and pestle beside the oven, and began to prepare a meal of grain. "Well, he is a most gentle man," she said, nodding. "I am certain that the Lord *will* bless him."

Naomi could not help but notice Ruth's fallen countenance, and wondered what to make of it. "My dear," she inquired, "how did you fare in the field, aside from your labors? Were folks kind to you?"

The girl had not intended to speak of the assault, but was grateful now to discuss something besides Boaz. "There was an incident, Mother, which frightened me."

Naomi drew close, listening anxiously. "Yes—what happened?" she urged.

"A man set upon me. . . . No, he did not have his way."

"Oh, my child!" the matron cried. "I warned you. . . . "

"Yes, Mother. So you did."

"And Boaz?" she prodded. "Was he informed of this?"

"He was," Ruth replied, her eyes clouding. "He was very good to me from that moment. He is a generous person, as you can see," she said, pointing to the crocks of grain. "He would have treated any woman so well."

The young widow's voice was dramatically unfeeling as she affirmed this. Naomi studied her rigid movements as she prepared the barley flour, and asked no more questions.

"Furthermore," Ruth added, with tense insistence, "when I left the field today, Boaz said to me, 'You should stay close to my servants until they have finished *all* my harvest.' "

The elder was not blind or deaf. It took no more for her to see that the girl's emotions ran high on the subject of the landowner. Suddenly she recalled the handsome horseman whom Ruth had watched from the rooftop. Of course, that must have been Boaz! Few others in Bethlehem would fit the description. And though she did not like to admit it, she need not have it spelled out on parchment that her daughter-in-law was in love.

A span of awkward minutes passed, before Naomi tried to ease the tension. "Well," she said, clearing her throat, "it is good, my daughter, that you go out with his maids, lest others fall upon you in the field."

"Yes," Ruth replied, a bit too agreeably. "It is good."

CHAPTER
FOURTEEN

The next few days, as Ruth worked the barley harvest, and as she was thrown repeatedly into her master's company, a peculiar thing began to happen to her mind. Memories of Mahlon and images of Boaz began to merge.

This troubled her greatly, mixing guilt with fear.

True, the two men were similar enough in appearance that, on a purely physical level, such a thing was not so odd. Mahlon had told her of Elimelech's two older brothers. Boaz was the son of the second eldest, and was, therefore, first cousin to Mahlon. So, of course there was a strong family resemblance.

But, in Ruth's unbidden imaginings, the overlapping was deeper, making her fear for her own character. After all, should not a wife retain the memory of her departed husband in sacrosanct purity? Surely Naomi preserved Elimelech in this way.

It was evening across the grain country. Ruth stood up from her gleaning and rubbed the small of her aching back. Smoke rose from piles of chaff and stubble being burned near the threshing floor outside Bethlehem. The elevated plateau had been used for generations as a convenient place for reapers to take their harvest on its last stop to market. Here gentle Mediterranean breezes met with hot blasts from Syria, producing a perfect winnowing wind. And from late afternoon until just before dark, the flat hill was abustle with activity.

This evening the wind carried ash from the chaff piles up toward Jebus, whose walls peeked over the distant Hinnom ridge. Ruth's gaze followed the smoky haze until it mingled with the twilight of the northern mountains, and she remembered what Naomi had said concerning the heathen city situated there.

Had Ruth ever borne a son, she would have taught him such things — that Israel belonged to God, and that what God had promised Abraham belonged to Israel. Surely if the Jews ever had a king, he should reign in the courts once occupied by Melchizedek — the courts of Jebus, once called Salem. And surely a temple fit for Jehovah should grace its highest rise.

She also remembered what Naomi had told her regarding "Messiah." All the legends and prophecies of the Hebrews were a mystery, but Ruth loved them with her whole heart. Even now, she considered the young women who worked the land about her, and wondered if one of them might someday bear the "Anointed One."

As for herself, she was only a daughter of Lot, Abraham's dispossessed nephew. And though, by now, she did quite literally "bear the dust of Israel in her veins," for Ruth and all her kin it seemed there was no place in history.

As she pondered this, a rider approached through the field. With warm greetings he addressed the sheave-maidens: "Grace be with you, daughters of Judah!"

"And with you," they returned, waving and eyeing each other with rapturous sighs.

It was Boaz. Ruth could not constrain a little stab of jealousy when he stopped to converse with the girls.

But as he came on, drawing near to the Moabitess, she perceived again what she had always tried to discount—a special gleam in his eye at the sight of her.

Reaching down, he bid her join him. "You may beat out your grain with the reapers. I will take you to the threshing station," he offered. "Hand me your satchel and climb up."

Ruth's heart raced as she complied, taking his strong arm and mounting behind him. As Boaz spurred his horse to a gallop and headed toward Bethlehem, she glanced back at the sisterhood of the field.

Together they leaned in whispers, some smiling after her, but most watching with furrowed brows.

CHAPTER
FIFTEEN

Ever since Naomi had first detected Ruth's growing interest in Boaz, the old woman found herself strangled with resentment. She did not like to admit that she was so protective of Mahlon's memory, but she was.

With time on her hands, and in her self-imposed isolation, the resentment had blossomed and fed upon itself. And though she had not overtly expressed it to Ruth, it was already doing damage to their relationship.

She worked on the rooftop today, weaving a blanket upon her loom from yarn purchased by barter. Ruth's wages had been sufficient enough the past few days, that they had been able to exchange the grain for a variety of foodstuffs and sundries.

As she wove earthy ambers, golds, and rusts together, Naomi recalled the desert of Moab, and suddenly her resentment took another direction. She found herself, much to her astonishment, railing against Elimelech in her mind. In fact, her feelings against Ruth were strangely eclipsed by this new emotion, though she fought against it with all her might.

"But, I must honor his memory!" she rebuked herself.

Suddenly, those words echoed like thunder in her

mind, cracking it wide open. For they expressed the very sentiment she had subtly foisted off on her daughter-in-law. If she must, beyond question, honor the departed Elimelech, Ruth must honor Mahlon, to the point of thinking on no other man!

The irrationality of such presumption did not elude her. She knew she had no right to require such devotion of another.

Why then did she require it of Naomi? For indeed, she *had* required it of herself. Had not eligible Moab Jews come courting when she was out of her widow's veil? Yes—but she had refused them all.

"Because I love my husband," she had told them.

Now she wondered, fearfully wondered, if that had been the reason.

In truth, she saw it now, as she stood from her loom and traipsed the rooftop, rubbing her hands nervously together. She had taken no suitor after Elimelech's death, because. . . .

Her heart stopped.

Because she was full of guilt.

Recognition gripped her like a vice. This was the stranglehold upon her soul: guilt. For, beneath her mourning lay the fear that she had somehow caused his demise.

"Can unforgiveness kill?" she whispered, staring across the hills toward Jordan.

The question seemed almost to be voiced by another. And yet it was Naomi who posed it—the Naomi who not only feared she had brought about her husband's death, but whose spirit had long ago stripped itself of life.

She knew now that she had never forgiven

Elimelech for his decision to leave Judah. Though she had complied, she had never surrendered to his choice. Whether he had been right or wrong, she had not released him from going against her will in the matter.

The devoted widow, the one whom everyone praised for her selfless loyalty, could hide no longer from the truth. It had risen like an acrid odor from her heart, and had seeped through her pores for years — suffocating those who drew too near.

Indeed, had she not even sent her two sons away on their last day, fully aware of her disapproval? They had not violated the name of their father, as she had accused them. They had violated *her,* by their independence. But she had chosen to wave the banner of the voiceless dead before them — a shroud to cloak them in the grave.

Furthermore, had she not subconsciously determined to keep Ruth from fulfillment, once the girl had decided to abide with her? She — who had once urged the young widow to stay behind in Moab, to seek a new husband for herself.

And what of Elimelech? How the man had suffered in her cold embrace all his days in Moab! The bride of his youth had turned from him, giving him duty, but no affection.

So, of course, she had needed to keep him alive, in her memory if nowhere else. Though he became a specter, a haunting phantom, she could not let him go.

"Forgive me, my husband!" she cried, lifting a fist to her forehead. "As it has been done unto you, so be it unto me!"

Naomi had lost track of time. It was well past sunset when she recovered. And when she entered the present, she found herself beside Elimelech's potting wheel, in the dark corner of the court.

Her cheeks were wet with remorse, and she was sitting in a huddle when Ruth came upon her.

"Mother," the girl cried, racing to her with open arms. "What is it?" She knelt beside Naomi and held her tight. "Has something happened?" she implored.

"God, forgive me," the matron was whispering, again and again.

Ruth drew her to her feet and led her to rest beside the fountain. Dipping the tip of her own veil into the cool, splashing water, she proceeded to wash the woman's face.

Gradually the sobs subsided, and the old widow leaned back, her eyes closed. "I have violated the living and the dead," she groaned. "I killed my husband, and I would have suffocated you, my daughter."

Ruth was horrified. "What are you saying, Mother? No one killed Elimelech!"

"My hard heart robbed him of life. I murdered him as surely as with my two hands!" the matron declared.

The daughter-in-law knew the woman raved, and yet she felt she must address the issue.

"Dear lady," Ruth spoke calmly, "I know not what troubles you. But you have taught me well. And now you must heed your own teachings."

Naomi looked up doubtfully and trembled.

"Listen, Mother," the girl began. "You spoke kindly these words to me, upon the death of my beloved Mahlon: 'Your husband was a friend of God. All lovers of Jehovah share in the world to come.' Now," Ruth insisted, "if Jehovah has his hand upon Elimelech this moment, did he not own and protect him in life?"

"Perhaps," Naomi sighed. "But. . . . "

"No 'perhaps,' " Ruth interrupted. " 'God gives,' you once told me, 'and God takes away. Blessed be the name of the Lord.' His life and death were not in *your* hands. No — my lady! If you have done anything amiss, it is in refusing to let him go. Forgive yourself! I am certain that Elimelech has long since forgiven you."

The elder woman smarted under the correction. But studying the girl's intelligent green eyes, she read the compassion in them, and with a sigh, shook her head. "Truly, your parents named you aright," she said. "You are a 'woman's friend.' "

The Moabitess only smiled. "Now, then," she commanded, standing, "rise up, and let us fetch some supper."

Naomi still reeled from the exhortation, but grasping Ruth by the hand, pulled her back. "First," she pleaded, " tell me . . . did you see Boaz today?"

"I did," the girl replied, wondering at the sudden reference to the much-avoided topic.

"And he is well?" Naomi inquired.

"He is, Mother. Why do you ask?"

The elder rose up, her eyes atwinkle with new life. "I am only curious," she said, shuffling toward the pantry. "Only curious."

CHAPTER
SIXTEEN

Until recently, Naomi had not been to town since she and Ruth entered the city. Suddenly, her urge to be with other women and to pass time in friendly conversation was insatiable.

This afternoon she would spend hours at market, as she had each day for a week, and tomorrow she would do likewise—and the next day, until, by wheat harvest, she would become a fixture of the village square.

This was the Naomi whom everyone remembered—Naomi, "sweet and pleasant." Even her appearance had altered, her expression and vitality. She seemed, in fact, to grow younger.

How much this metamorphosis was due to renewed interest in cosmetics, combs, and adornment, and how much would have come about naturally with her changed outlook, no one could say. But at least ten years had melted from her in a short time.

She and Abigail spent much time together laughing about a hundred things. For truly, the widow had now come home—not to die, but to live.

And she had much to live for. Naomi had a dream, and used each waking minute plotting its fulfillment.

Daily, she waited for the proper moment, baffling Ruth with inquisitions regarding her master, Boaz, and his doings. She watched the grain market, keeping track of events of the field, and calculating the execution of her plan.

The daughter-in-law knew that more than Naomi's personal liberation, more than freedom of soul, lay behind her exuberance. Had Ruth not known this she would have feared for her mind now as much as she once had. For Naomi was possessed by peculiar outbursts of laughter and private giggles. Giddiness had replaced depression, and a near-girlish impulsiveness had overcome lethargy. But, for all this, the daughter could only be grateful. She knew that whatever had given the woman hope, it was better than the living death which had once drained her.

The matron scurried home from the bazaar on the hottest day of the year, glad that Ruth was in the fields and not in the empty house. She had purchased a sackful of fruits and vegetables, cool and in season, as well as a good-sized mackerel from the coastal waters. She set the food on the fountain bench and bustled upstairs to Ruth's gallery room.

Somewhat ill at ease invading this private sanctum, she shrugged off the feeling and reasoned that she was here for a good cause. She stepped gingerly toward the closet and surveyed the many colorful gowns hung there upon a dozen hooks. Tebit had done well by Ruth, providing her with the finest of clothing—cloaks and tunics for which the poor girl had had little use since leaving Moab. But Naomi was looking for one gown in particular, and when she found it, she laughed aloud.

"Oops!" she caught herself, wondering for whose benefit these audible slips came these days.

Out of habit, she looked about the room, fully expecting to sense Elimelech's presence. But she was realizing, gradually, that the phantom she had perceived so many years had been a conjuring born of her own guilt. As Ruth had said, Elimelech belonged with God, and she must release him.

Therefore, since her own release, he came no more.

Surely he would approve, however, of her actions this day. She could continue to honor him in a healthy way, by turning her interests to the future.

So, it was with delight that she lifted the emerald sari from its hook—the garment prepared for celebration of Mahlon's good fortune—the gown never worn.

Tenderly she laid it across the girl's bed and fumbled in her closet again for a pair of sandals. Pale scuffs of fine calfskin were placed beside the green tunic, along with assorted neck chains and bracelets retrieved from small boxes on the dressing table. After seeing that Ruth's jars of ointments and cosmetics were arranged for easy access, she hurried downstairs.

Naomi then set about to prepare a feast—the first full meal she had tackled since arriving in Bethlehem. And as she worked, she hummed a tune, having taken up psalms again.

"My heart is steadfast, O God," she put words to the melody. "I will sing praises even with my soul. I waited patiently for the Lord, and he inclined unto me, and heard my cry. He put a new song in my mouth, a hymn of praise to our God!"

Because it was such a warm day, only the fish would be cooked. The rest of the supper, the fruits and vegetables, would be sliced fresh and shade-cooled; arranged on platters which had been kept frigid beneath the fountain.

When Ruth arrived, depleted by her labors under the sun, she looked with amazement on the fare spread before her. Lowering her heavy satchel to the floor, she cried, "Mother! Did *you* do all this? Nothing has ever looked so good!"

Naomi escorted her to a pillow beside the floor-linen upon which were arrayed the delicacies. She sat down gratefully, and the matron removed her dusty sandals, served her a platter of food, and proceeded to wash her feet.

Never had the mother-in-law performed such service for the girl, and Ruth could only comply speechlessly.

When the daughter had been satisfied, and when she was relaxed, the elder woman explained the purpose of the celebration.

"Child," she began, kneeling before her, "you have sacrificed a great deal for me. But you are young, and you must not think to give up your entire future for my sake. Should I not do what I can to seek security for you?"

Ruth was attentive, wondering what she could be leading to. And with the mention, again, of her beloved's name, her heart surged.

"Is not Boaz our kinsman?" Naomi said. "Now listen to me. In Israel, as in your country, we have the tradition of the 'goel.'"

Ruth was incredulous. According to the custom of the "goel," or "redeemer," upon a man's death, the nearest brother would marry his surviving spouse, in order, as they said, "to raise up a son to him, that his

230

name perish not from the earth." While the law was
hazy in both nations regarding the necessity of any
kinsman beyond a brother filling in, it was true that
the nearest relative was to redeem a childless man's
property, and was usually expected, with it, to take
the wife as his own.

But never had it occurred to Ruth that Boaz could
perform such service. As she listened to Naomi's
plan, her head spun.

"As you know," the matron went on, "I still have the
parcel of land which Elimelech left me. We do need
money, and we must sell it. We have the right to ask a
kinsman to purchase it."

Ruth shook herself. There was too much to consider here. "Mother," she objected, "I would not wish
for Boaz to marry me out of obligation!"

Naomi drew back, slapping her hands upon her
thighs. "Of course you wouldn't!" she agreed. "I am
only thinking of every benefit we can incur from our
rights as widows."

Ruth was confounded and wished to think upon
this, but Naomi was under the stress of some
urgency.

"Listen well," she said again. "I was in the market
today, and there is much talk of the weather and what
the landowners are going to do about it. There will
not be much dew on this hot night, and the fields will
be workable. So to insure the bulk of the harvest and
to protect it from any fire which could spring up, the
managers are requiring many reapers to work
through till morning."

Ruth nodded her head. "I heard rumors to that
effect. But none of the gleaners were informed."

"Gleaners," the elder reminded her, "are not privy to such decisions. I certainly would not have known had I not insisted on it."

The girl studied Naomi with amazement. Never had she seen the woman so ambitious for anything, and she knew she dare not question her.

"Furthermore," she continued, "I learned that the owners will be working beside their servants to get the harvest in. Behold, now, Boaz himself will be winnowing barley tonight at the threshing floor."

Ruth feared the implications. Part of her did not wish to hear the proposal, but she listened nonetheless with tense intrigue.

"Now, therefore, rise up," Naomi commanded. "Wash yourself, anoint yourself, put on your best garment, and go to the threshing floor tonight. Do all that I tell you, and it will go well for you. . . . "

CHAPTER
SEVENTEEN

All-night harvests were not unusual in Palestine. But
when conditions demanded them, they were used for
celebration as well as hard work.

Especially at the threshing station, where the
profits of labor could be seen firsthand, there was an
atmosphere of gaiety.

Since Bethlehem's threshing floor was publicly,
rather than privately owned, it was a community
gathering place, many folk turning out for the activi-
ties accompanying such an evening. Men of all
trades, who understood that their city's economy
thrived on the grain industry, worked in shifts alongside the regular winnowers, and the air was filled
with a festive spirit. In return for their voluntary
help, they received sacks of free grain, and a few
hours of pure enjoyment.

Wine flowed freely at such events — intoxicating
wine as well as the traditional chomets. Musicians
and dancers often joined the workers, supplying en-
tertainment and enough singing to dispel weariness
and maintain enthusiasm.

But it was a distinctly masculine event. No woman
was supposed to be present, and even female winnowers of the harvest were sent home before dark
descended. For it was a rowdy occasion, an evening

when male camaraderie dominated, and no lady would feel at ease.

As Ruth crept through the "needle's eye," the small exit left open at night beside the locked city gate, she felt very conspicuous. Though no one was nearby, she paused to look behind when she stepped into the darkness beyond Bethlehem. From across the low plain which led toward fields and hills, she could discern the sound of music, and even the low rumble of men's laughter was carried on the wind.

An anxious chill pricked her skin, and she would have gone no further, had Naomi's insistent command not hounded her. "On nights like this, the landlords sleep at the threshing station," the woman had explained, "to protect the grain from robbers. Do not make yourself known to Boaz until he has finished eating and drinking. And when he goes to lie down, notice the place where he rests."

Ruth drew her tapestry veil over her shoulders, the finest one her father had ever made, and she shuddered, remembering the rest of Naomi's directions. "And when he has reclined, go and uncover his feet and lie down. Then . . . he will tell you what you shall do."

Scarcely could she believe, now, that she had consented to such a thing. But Naomi *was* the head of the house. And Ruth had committed herself to the woman—to go where she went, lodge where she lodged, and make her people her own. In other words, she was her servant, and short of agreeing to starve with her, rather than go glean, she would give due honor.

Still, the prospect of compliance was fearsome.

Might not the master's first introduction to her, as the victim of sexual assault, incline him to doubt Ruth's motives? It was highly possible that he would construe the action she planned tonight as tantamount to whorish solicitation. Had Jehovah brought her to this land to bear disrepute?

She stood in the shadow of the gate a long time, weighing the matter. Perhaps, after all, Naomi *was* mad. But enough of her reasoning was sane that it gave Ruth courage.

Indeed, it would not be wrong to request Boaz to keep the "goel," and there might never again be opportunity to approach him.

These facts in mind, Ruth began her journey toward the elevated rock crowned by the threshing station.

A dozen chaff-fires about the base of the mesa illumined it like a cone of shining gold. Atop the plateau could be seen the silhouettes of the winnowers, bent over the stalks with flails, or tossing masses of straw toward the perpetual wind with broad wooden shovels and crook-pronged forks. As Ruth drew near, trying to watch her steps across the rutty fields, she could distinguish the laborers from the partygoers, the dancers and revelers from those on shift.

Suddenly, as the firelight reflected off her gown in an orange sheen, she remembered Mahlon. How strange it was to be wearing the dress prepared just for his praise, in quest of a new husband. It was not guilt she felt, but a terrible sadness—a lingering grief at the loss of her first love.

However, she reminded herself that, according to the customs of Palestine and Transjordan, she would be securing hope than an heir could be raised up for Mahlon—that, in a very real way, his name would be preserved in the earth.

How fully the people of Israel and nearby nations believed this was shown by the fact that the son of the new union would actually bear the surname of the deceased, and would be written into the legal records as his offspring. There was to be no possessiveness on the part of the kinsman-redeemer toward that child, though he was expected to raise him as his own in every other way, and should love him with the love of a father.

As Ruth contemplated this, she smiled happily. If she could please Mahlon in such a way, she would do so.

Quickly she approached the plateau, her heart beating in rhythm with the dancers' drums. The flat terraces of the threshing mount, illumined in the firelight, and imbued with otherworldliness by the sound of flutes and lyres, reminded her of Moab. How similar the scene was to the Chemoshite temple on celebration nights, its gold terraces fraught with flame, and its courtiers spinning to hypnotic tunes!

But there was no horror in this place, no reason to flee.

Suddenly Ruth embraced her purpose with zeal. If she were to live in Israel, let her take all she could claim . . . for Mahlon, for Naomi, and . . . for herself.

It was close to midnight when Ruth set foot atop the threshing floor. Though the revelers were focused on their party and the workers on their winnowing, she

did not wish to risk being seen, and so settled down
behind a grain pile at the edge of the plateau.

Peering above the heap, she tried to locate Boaz.

It was not difficult to spy him. He stood head and
shoulders above most men present, and his very demeanor, as always, set him apart.

At the moment, he was being summoned to repair
the ox-driven machine used to separate kernels from
husks. It seemed to have gotten hung up on something, so that the beasts could not budge it.

Ruth watched privately as he soothed the anxious
creatures, who were yoked side by side, and as he
surveyed the underpinnings of the iron-toothed
planks which they dragged behind them.

Finding that the chains which attached the har-
nesses to the weighted board had become tangled, he
quickly unraveled the mess and stood up, prodding
the oxen into contented action.

His torso, bare to the waist, glistened with sweat in
the gold light, and as he turned to his servants,
directing them to throw more grain beneath the machine, he displayed unrivaled authority.

Though there were other landowners here, men of
all classes looked to him for leadership.

But he was not above the most common work. No
longer needed at the machine, he joined a young
fellow who was filling a wide, flat basket with chaff,
and together they lifted it, swinging it back and forth
like a giant sieve, while grain fell through to a sifted
pile. It was a heavy object, laden with several bushels
of material. Ruth admired Boaz's strength, outlined
in defined muscles and hardened thighs.

When the great round basket had been emptied,

the master and the young man stepped to the edge of the threshing floor and cast the remaining chaff to the wind. Away it was carried to the dark field below, where it would be raked up and burned.

Boaz had probably labored nonstop since morning. Except for routine breaks, his day had been full.

Ruth observed him breathlessly as he went to the water pails lined up beneath a central tarpaulin. In the dim light of the tent's lantern, he ran his hands through the liquid and washed his face vigorously, pouring yet more of the water through his silver-streaked hair and then stepping into the breeze.

His mantle over his shoulders, he joined the party for a few moments, partaking of the dark loaves provided, and thus keeping the proverb, "Beware of eating fine bread and giving black bread to your servants."

Ruth watched their laughing interchanges, and her anxiety mounted as she wondered how long it might be before he retired.

The wineskin had been passed for the third time. Boaz was well relaxed and his heart merry. Soon he rose and the girl drew back behind the grain pile, peering out carefully, as he stretched and yawned in the moonlight.

"The Lord be with you," he called to his comrades as he walked toward the shadows.

"And with you!" they returned. "Sleep well, our brother!"

Though Boaz certainly could have provided himself with a comfortable bed, he was not above the other proverb which warned masters not to sleep on feathers, while their servants slept on straw. He

would rest at the end of a wheat pile tonight, and
would be available should any emergency arise.

Ruth's pulse quickened as she watched him select
the very heap behind which she was hidden.

Boaz lay down upon the matted straw which was
there, gathering some together as a pillow, and using
his large cloak as a blanket.

Within moments the man was asleep, his chest rising and falling in gentle, even breathing.

Cautiously, Ruth stepped out from the pile and
secretly approached him. For a moment she studied
him in the moonlight, the music fading from her consciousness as he became her full focus.

How glorious he was, in the prime of life and the
vigor of his manhood! Her heart tripped fearfully as
she considered just who he was. Suddenly, she felt
the foolishness of her venture—that she, a mere
foreigner, a woman without station or means, could
think he would even hear her request! Why, Boaz
could have any suntanned damsel of the field. Who
was she to compete with them?

Almost she turned to flee, to put all thought of the
ridiculous plan behind her. But then she remembered
Naomi's command, and Boaz's kind attentions.

Bending low, she uncovered his feet and lay down,
drawing herself beneath his cloak and curling up
quietly beside him.

Hours passed. But she did not sleep, as she
listened to the muted revelry at the far end of the
floor, and to the sounds of those who worked through
the night.

Any movement Boaz made in his sleep sent an
alarm through her. But he did not wake.

It was the middle of the darkest hours when she, at last close to dozing, inadvertently rested her head upon his thigh.

Startled, Boaz sat bolt upright, flinging his cloak aside, and bending forward.

Ruth, rising upon one elbow, looked into his bewildered face, and felt the blood rush to her cheeks.

"Who are you?" he gasped, his tone half angry.

"I am Ruth . . . your maid," she stammered, wondering now why she had ever risked this escapade. And then, hardly believing her own ears, she said, "So spread your mantle over your maid, for you are a close relative."

Silence hung between them, broken only by the rustling of sheaves as the wind swept up from the plain. Ruth had, in essence, asked Boaz to marry her—for bethrothal was signified by a man covering his beloved with his cloak, a symbol of protection and cherishing.

Ruth could see his face in the blue light of harvest moon. At first, she could not interpret his expression, for it seemed vacant of emotion. As he spoke, however, the words coming soft and low, she realized that his strange countenance bespoke wonder and speechless respect.

"May you be blessed of the Lord, my daughter," he replied. "This kindness you are showing is greater than that which you have shown Naomi, for you come after *me,* rather than younger men, whether poor or rich."

Ruth sighed, overwhelmed with gratitude, and she bowed herself to the ground, grasping his feet and holding them close.

Boaz reached for her and lifted her up, drawing her close to his bosom. There he enfolded her in his arms, his heart surging.

"Do not fear, my daughter," he whispered. "I will do for you whatever you ask, for all my people in the city know that you are a woman of excellence."

Ruth sank into his embrace willingly, pulling her knees up beside him. For a long while he sat and held her, calming her and reassuring her without a word.

But then, a sullen thought seemed to overtake him, and his hold became more determined. Ruth peered into his face, afraid to ask the cause of this change. "Now," he said in a somber tone, "it is true that I am a close relative. However," his voice broke off and he took a deep breath. "however, there is one closer than I."

One closer than Boaz? Ruth knew of no other kinsman. Her pulse sped as the implications flooded over her. "But, who, my lord . . . ?"

Boaz only shook his head, silencing the girl. And as he went on, her mind clouded with a dozen dreadful speculations.

"Remain this night," he was pleading, his very insistence confirming her fears, "and when morning comes, if he will redeem you . . . good—let him redeem you."

Here he paused, reading her sudden tenseness carefully. He seemed to take comfort in her reaction, and drew her head to his shoulder once again, stroking her brow with a strong hand.

"But if he does not wish to redeem you," he went on, "then I will do so."

He did not tell her that he could not imagine any man denying such an opportunity. He did not tell her that he feared she would prefer the younger man.

Ruth warmed to the sounds of his words, her body conforming to his embrace. As he sensed her tender response, he gained confidence and lifted her face to his.

"As the Lord lives, I will perform this," he swore.

Ruth smiled up at him, and as he tucked his cloak about her shoulders, he bid her stretch out beside him.

"Lie down until morning," he said, "but rise before dawn—and let no one know that a woman came to the threshing floor."

PART IV
Harvest

How great is thy goodness,
Which thou has stored up for those who fear thee.
Which thou has wrought for those who take refuge in
  thee. . . .

PSALM 31:19
A Psalm of David
(Author's paraphrase)

CHAPTER ONE

It was just sunup when Ruth returned home. Upon her back, like a great bag, was her tapestry veil, full of wheat which the master had given her.

Naomi ran to the door the instant she heard her hand upon the latch. The elder woman had not slept all night for anticipation.

"How did it go, my daughter?" she cried, rubbing her hands together anxiously.

"He *is* a very kind man," Ruth replied, a twinkle dancing in her eye. "Very kind, indeed!"

"He agreed!" Naomi spurred her.

When Ruth nodded, the matron spun about like a small child doing a little jig. "Praise Jehovah!" she sang. "The Lord is faithful to the widow and the poor!"

"Yes," Ruth laughed, showing her the grain-heavy mantle. "He gave me these six measures of barley, saying, 'Do not go to your mother-in-law empty-handed.' "

"Bride-price!" Naomi deduced. "He fully intends to marry you!"

"Truly," Ruth said, "and to purchase the land you have to sell."

"Yes?" the woman marveled.

"Before I left this morning, he vowed to do so."

But then the girl glanced away, her face suddenly fallen.

The mother, who was sensitive to her every nuance of expression, caught her by the arm. "There is more you have not told me, my daughter."

"Yes," Ruth acknowledged. "I fear to repeat it."

Naomi drew her to the fountain and they sat down. "Speak," she commanded.

"It seems there is a kinsman closer than Boaz," Ruth explained, her heart nearly breaking with the words.

The elder woman was perplexed, weighing the message with care. "I know of no one, daughter. Elimelech had only two brothers, and the eldest moved far from here, with his children, well into the famine. A kinsman must abide in the same town to incur the full duty of redeemership."

Ruth shrugged her shoulders, tears brimming in her eyes, and Naomi touched her face lightly, reading the trembling of her lip.

"Wait, my daughter," she tried to comfort her. And then, studying her perfect features and emerald eyes, she whispered, "Boaz cannot help but love you. Wait until you know how the matter turns out. For he will not rest until he has settled it today."

It was still dawn-cool in the shade of Bethlehem's gate as Boaz paced the council court. He had entered town shortly after Ruth had departed the threshing floor, and was determined to meet with the elders the moment they convened.

He also had his eyes set for a certain fellow, whom he hoped would be passing this way soon.

When the reapers and winnowers who had not worked the night harvest began filtering through the gate on their way to the remaining tasks, he scanned each group carefully.

By mid-morning, when the traffic was thickening, the daily council was also gathering in the small, grassy area just inside the wall.

Boaz's pulse quickened as he saw the time draw near for his pronouncement, and he studied the passing reapers tenaciously. It seemed most of them had gone by already. He could not have missed the fellow, surely.

But, then of course, the one for whom he waited was an itinerant, bonded to no particular employer. Often tardy to work, he was a sluggard when he did put in his hours. In fact, Ben Salmon had not seen him in his own field since early barley harvest, and now wondered if the fellow had left the village.

Boaz's lip curled, and he walked to the edge of the council court, sitting down to wait.

The rabbis were already engaged in conversation when he joined them. They had great respect for Ben Salmon, but eyed him curiously, stroking their long white beards and whispering together.

"Brother," one of them said at last, "did you have a matter to bring before the elders?"

Boaz, preoccupied with reviewing the pedestrians, focused quickly on the speaker. "Sir, I do. It involves another brother, and I wait for him to come this way."

The rabbi, wondering at his intense demeanor, stepped aside and asked no more. But the patriarchs, clustering at his back, began to watch the road with him.

Meanwhile, three other pairs of eyes, all female, surveyed both the street and the council court with anxiety at least equal to Boaz's. Since Ruth had set the matter out, Naomi had determined not to miss a syllable of the brewing drama.

Abigail's balcony, she recalled, directly overlooked the court. That energetic purveyor of local news would surely want to follow these developments, and would welcome her cousins to a front row seat.

The three women stood just inside the archway of the elevated porch, concealing themselves from view.

As Boaz waited, folk in the market and passersby noticed the elders' watchful mood. Gradually, a sizable crowd collected, murmuring and milling about.

At last, Ben Salmon spied the one for whom he had waited, and stood up, clearing his throat and hailing him.

"Turn aside, friend," he called. "Sit down here."

His voice bore a peculiar bite, the word "friend" spoken with an edge. And when Ruth peered out to see the newcomer, her breath came in a jolt.

"What is it?" Naomi asked. "Do you know this man?"

Did she *know* him? She would always live with the memory of his leering face and hot breath.

"Mother, he is the one whom I encountered my first day in the field!"

The matron leaned out from the arch, and viewing him, shook her head. "A near kinsman?" she gasped. "Are you certain?"

"I can never forget him," Ruth replied, her back rigid.

Naomi, caring not now who saw her, stepped to the

edge of the balcony and studied the reaper. Suddenly, she recognized him and her heart sank. Somehow she had never pictured him as a grown man. He had been barely older than Mahlon when she and her family had left Bethlehem. And whenever she had thought of him over the intervening years, it had been as her son's troublemaking playmate.

But had not his father, Elimelech's eldest brother, left this city long ago? To her knowledge the man had never returned, nor had his children.

Boaz was speaking again, however, and Ruth drew close behind her mother-in-law, anxiously watching the proceedings.

The handsome landowner had gathered the elders, ten in all, in a circle. "Sit down," he requested, pointing them to the stone benches surrounding their little conference area.

The milling crowd ceased its movement and listened intently.

Turning to the bewildered reaper, Boaz studied him coolly.

"Good sirs," he began, directing the council's attention to the newcomer, "this is Lehi, son of my father's eldest brother, Micah. He returned to Bethlehem early this year, seeking employment in my barley field. He asked that I keep his identity close, as his father and mine were rivals, and a shame it was for him to be my servant."

At this the spectators whispered yet the more and murmured among themselves.

"To this I agreed," Boaz explained, "but I refused to indenture him as he is a close kinsman. 'I shall keep your identity close,' I promised, 'if you act as an itinerant and be not bound to me.' "

Lehi shuffled nervously, wondering why now, at the end of harvest, Boaz was breaking his trust. He glared at the wondering crowd and turned toward the master angrily, his fist clenched.

Ruth tensed, fearing his next move, but Lehi respected the council and said nothing.

"I am forced to retract my silence," Boaz went on, "because a matter of greater urgency has arisen." Begging the council's indulgence, he said, "It regards the widow of our fathers' youngest brother, Elimelech. May I bring the matter forth?"

The elders, their interest piqued, nodded. "Proceed," the chairman directed. "We will hear the case."

Turning to the cousin, Boaz continued. "Naomi, who has come back from the country of Moab, has to sell the parcel of land which belonged to our uncle Elimelech," he announced. "So I thought to inform you, as you, being the son of the eldest brother, are the nearest relative. It was my obligation to tell you, and it is your duty to buy it before those sitting here and before the elders of my people."

As the itinerant listened, Ben Salmon scrutinized him carefully. To his surprise, the man showed no uneasiness at this request, and Boaz, knowing he had always been an unmoneyed man, wondered why. But he went on, "If you will redeem it, redeem it. But if not, tell me, that I may know. For, there is no one but you to redeem it and I am after you."

The crowd leaned together again, recalling the bitterness which had long existed between the two men's families, and the councilmen shook their heads. Having set the issue out, Boaz sighed deeply, assuming that his obligation regarding this kinsman was done. Once Lehi showed publicly that he could ill afford to purchase the property, he could step into his place, even to the taking of Ruth.

However, no one was prepared for the man's response. And when he spoke, fear flooded the women on the balcony.

"I will redeem the land," Lehi said simply.

Boaz's heart stopped in mid-beat, and Ruth clutched Naomi's hand. The elder widow, leaning over the balcony, drew back and held her daughter close.

"I am sorry to disappoint you, Ben Salmon," Lehi laughed, a gleam in his eye. "I know you could have used the field of Elimelech, seeing as how you have so little real estate."

The landowner's jaw tightened, and the congregation hung on his response.

"I was not going out to work today," the kinsman explained. "In fact my satchel is full of food for a journey to Ephraim. I received word last night that my father has passed away. And I go to claim my inheritance. Just think," he said with a triumphant smile, "how the timing has fallen to my advantage! Why, yesterday I could not have afforded your offer. But now I can," he said grinning. "And Elimelech's field will serve me well to redeem my father's claim in Bethlehem and reestablish his name in this place."

Tears welled in Ruth's eyes as she saw her destiny written plainly on the air. As Mahlon's widow, she was, by tradition, to be included with the land, as part of the redemption. In a rapidly moving blur, images of her future as this fellow's wife flashed before her, and she began to tremble.

Abigail held her by the elbow and Naomi embraced her about the waist, but neither had a word of hope.

Boaz, however, was not to be undone. Quickly, his mind sorted through the legal implications of Lehi's redemption, and spreading his feet in a solid stance, he challenged him.

"Cousin," he declared, "think not to raise up the name of your father on Elimelech's land. For his son Mahlon had a wife." Here his eyes traveled to the balcony, where he knew Ruth watched him. As their gazes locked, her face grew flush, and her throat dry. Helplessly she listened as he matter-of-factly gave her away. "On the day you buy the field from the hand of Naomi, you must also acquire Ruth the Moabitess, widow of the deceased," he was saying, "in order to raise up in the name of Mahlon his inheritance."

Ruth's head spun. What could Boaz be thinking, to release her so coolly to this stranger?

But she did not know Lehi as Boaz knew him, and as Mahlon, even as a child, had known him.

Lehi followed Boaz's gaze, and now his own heart stood still.

At the sight of the girl, whom he had coveted from the moment he knew she had belonged to his enemy, Mahlon, he froze. Ruth's pure beauty had enraged him the first time he saw her, and now her innocent presence shot him through with self-recrimination.

Looking at the ground, he suddenly stammered, "I . . . . I do not know yet how much my father left me."

Boaz stepped close and pressed him. "Speak up,

man. Will you redeem the land and the lady?"

"I said," Lehi repeated, his face burning, "I do not yet know the sum of my inheritance. Perhaps it will not cover the price of the property."

Boaz looked down on the kinsman with disgust. "Why, Lehi, you know how poverty-stricken Naomi has been. I am certain you can have the parcel for a song. And then," he said, pointing to Ruth, "you may enjoy the fruits of Mahlon's death to the full."

The Moabitess shuddered as Lehi continued to stare at the ground. "I cannot redeem it for myself," he said shakily, "lest I jeopardize my own inheritance. Redeem it for yourself, my brother. You may have my right of redemption, for I cannot redeem it. Buy it for yourself."

Abigail and Naomi felt Ruth go limp in their hold as the breath escaped her. But the girl rallied quickly, her eyes fixed on Boaz.

As Lehi bent down to remove his sandal and give it to his cousin, signifying release of property rights, Naomi took Ruth by the hand, leading her to the street.

Quickly the matron rushed through the throng, drawing her daughter-in-law after, and coming directly between Lehi and Boaz.

It was not out of order for her to intercept the sandal as it was passed to the new redeemer. Grabbing it from Lehi, the elder woman sank to her knees and lifted it before Boaz.

"May you receive the property direct from Elimelech's hands," she cried, thrusting the shoe into Boaz's grasp. "May you not be forced to receive it from this man—for he is unclean."

The crowd marveled at the pronouncement, and Lehi turned contemptuous eyes on Ruth, knowing she had revealed him as her attacker.

"Unclean?" Boaz repeated. "How so, Naomi?"

"Lehi Ben Micah is the one who set upon my daughter in the field!"

The elders now pressed close to Boaz's back, staring over his shoulders at the guilt-faced itinerant.

"Is this so?" the master asked, his voice soft toward the Moabitess.

"It is, my lord," she conceded.

Boaz had once promised that if he were ever given the chance, he would vindicate Ruth against her attacker. Turning the sandal over and over in his hand, he at last made his judgment.

"I receive the redeemership, and all that pertains to Mahlon," he proclaimed, "but I return the sandal to Lehi. He will need it for his journey."

Wedging it between the kinsman's fingertips, he directed, "When you pass through the gate, my brother, do not seek ever to return. Continue your trip to Ephraim and stay there. For the name of your family is no longer welcome in Bethlehem."

Lehi, head down, did as he was commanded, not daring to look his countrymen in the eyes. And as he exited, a cheer went up from the crowd.

Boaz now focused full attention on the lovely girl who had captured his heart weeks before. Beckoning her to his side, he faced the elders and vowed, "You are witnesses today that I have bought from Naomi's hand all that belonged to Elimelech and all that belonged to Chilion and Mahlon. Moreover, I have acquired Ruth the Moabitess, widow of Mahlon, to be my wife in order to raise up the name of the deceased on his inheritance, that the name of the deceased be not cut off from his brothers or from the court of his birthplace. To all this, you are witnesses this day."

And all the people who were in the court, and the elders said, "We are witnesses. May the Lord make the woman who is coming into your home like Rachel and Leah, who built the house of Israel. And may you achieve wealth in Ephratah and fame in Bethlehem."

CHAPTER
TWO

Ruth would remember every pulsebeat, every little turn of the next few hours.

Upon receiving Boaz's vow, the city had gone wild. The bride, being an independent widow and not a virgin, was considered married with that simple ceremony, and had been ushered to Naomi's home by the women of the town, where they bathed her, coiffed her hair and painted her face with blossom stains, draped her in silks, girded her with glittering belts, and adorned her with jewels.

A holiday had been declared and all work in the fields ceased. Reapers, winnowers, and gleaners joined with tradesmen and elders at market square, while musicians and dancers filled the streets with revelry.

A wedding of any stature was an excuse for joy. But the wedding of a nobleman was reason for all labor and all sorrow to be set aside.

For eight hours the city feasted, and the wine flowed.

At evening, lanterns flooded the marketplace, and the marriage, which had begun with Boaz's quick proclamation, would not be consummated until all the people allowed it.

When the moment came that Ruth was escorted to Boaz's home, it was only the climax to frivolity which would fill the dark hours till morning.

Upon a tall, canopied camel she rode, surrounded by hundreds of laughing, singing folk. Up the steep slope beyond the wall, toward her husband's home she was carried, jostled by the celebrating masses, swayed to and fro atop the creature's decorated back.

When at last she stood with Boaz alone, watching from his chamber balcony as the crowd departed, she listened with awe to their benediction. "May your house be like the house of Perez whom Tamar bore to Judah," the people called, "through the sons which this young woman shall bear!"

Boaz reached out to touch Ruth's soft hand which gripped the balustrade, and he lifted her fingers to his lips. For a long time his gaze drifted through hers, and when the hill lay silent, he spoke.

"Dear girl, you barely know me."

Ruth smiled, her mouth trembling. "I know you well enough, my lord."

The gentle man caressed her face. "And what, pray tell, have you determined?" he asked.

Ruth peered toward the town wall and found the housetop from which she had first seen him.

"I watched you pace this very balcony my first evening in Bethlehem," she replied. "I know you have been a solitary and a lonely man."

Boaz sighed, dropping his eyes to the floor. "Your description is correct," he admitted. "I am a man of means and a man of Israel. But I have dwelt apart."

"You have many servants, my lord, many maids."

"Indeed," he answered, his expression wistful.

"And you could have had a hundred women," she added. "For what did you wait?"

Boaz pulled his bride close and rested his chin lightly on her head, staring out toward the star-studded heavens. "The timing of Jehovah," he said, "the hand of God."

Ruth listened respectfully and leaned onto his bosom. "Is the timing right?" she inquired.

The man smiled, stroking her forehead with his cheek. "When I saw you in the tent that first day, I saw the Lord's fulfillment."

Ruth raised her face to his, her eyes misting, as Boaz moved his hand down her side, toward her slender waist. Drawing the full length of her body close against him, he sighed a little.

"My lady," he said, "remember this—should you conceive tonight, the child shall be Mahlon's heir, but son of Boaz. And though you place the babe on Naomi's lap, it was Boaz who held you in his arms and made you his own."

Encircling her with his embrace, he swept her off the balcony and cradled her like a lamb against his heart.

Once inside his chamber, the music of the city and the lights of Bethlehem meant nothing. The memory of Moab and the sorrows of the past faded away.

Ruth knew only Boaz and the secret things of his love.

CHAPTER
THREE

There did come a day when Ruth placed a baby in Naomi's arms.

The elder woman had sat faithfully at her birthing bed all morning, as Boaz waited with the rabbis in Bethlehem's court. And all the matron's lady friends had lingered near the door of the chamber where Ruth travailed with child.

When the ruddy, black-haired infant had come squalling into the world, Elimelech's widow had served as midwife. And Ruth had, as tradition dictated, placed him in Naomi's keeping.

The child was to have two surnames. Before he had been born, it had been determined that he would be called Ben Mahlon *and* Ben Boaz.

And before Boaz would even be summoned to see the babe, Mahlon's mother would have selected his given name.

For by the custom cherished in Israel, this was Naomi's redeemer, the surety that her husband's line and her son's line would prevail.

In a circle, the city matrons joined hands at Ruth's bedside. Naomi, seated in the middle, tears brimming in her shining eyes, held the wriggling infant aloft.

Instantly the neighbor women began to chant, "Blessed is the Lord who has sent you a redeemer

today. And may his name become famous in Israel.
May he also be to you a restorer of life and a sustainer of your old age," they sang, "for your daughter-in-law, who loves you and is better to you than seven sons, has given birth to him!"

Abigail leaned close and whispered, "Naomi, place the child upon your lap."

The elder widow trembled, almost fearing the fulfillment. For to lay the babe upon her knees was to make him her own.

But when she looked cautiously at the young mother, and saw that Ruth smiled approvingly, the tears, which had only filled her eyes, now spilled over.

Drawing the child to her frail breast, she rested him in her lap, and threw her head back, laughing for joy.

"A son has been born to Naomi!" the women cried.

"Call him 'Obed'!" someone insisted.

The name was quickly passed around.

"Yes, 'Obed,' " they declared.

Naomi thought long on this, " 'Servant'?" she pondered. "Is that a fair designation?"

"He is Jehovah's gift, to serve and lift you up," they explained.

And so, the child was named.

Naomi returned him to Ruth's breast and stood up. "Call Boaz," she said, and all the women departed.

The master appeared at the chamber door, almost afraid to enter. Only when his young wife assured him that they were alone, did he approach her bed.

Ruth pulled back the covers, revealing the small

one who suckled there. And she drew her husband close.

"Though he is Mahlon's heir, my lord, he is your son," she whispered.

Boaz's eyes searched hers hesitantly, but as she spoke again, his heart soared.

"Though I placed him on Naomi's lap," she reminded him, "it was you who embraced me, and made me your own. He is a son of our love together."

CHAPTER
FOUR

When Naomi had been released from the guilt which
had hounded her after Elimelech's death, her first response had been to take up singing again. The sweet
psalms which had always revived her once more
filled her home.

With the advent of Ruth's marriage and the coming
of Naomi's first grandchild, the songs had multiplied.
And they wove themselves into the consciousness of
Mahlon's thriving heir.

Familiar they were to Ruth, as well, and should
Naomi not live to see the next generation, the
daughter-in-law would pass them on.

Over the remaining years of the widow's life, she
divided her time between the village estate and
Boaz's majestic home beyond the wall. Due to the
nobleman's kindness, she was maintained in comfort,
and was considered as much his mother as Ruth's.

The Moabitess would never forget the conversation
of one afternoon when she stopped at Naomi's house
from a day of shopping. The elder woman had agreed
to watch little Obed while the young mother was at
market.

As Ruth had entered the court of the old home, her
heart had quickened to a delightful sound mixing
with the fountain's melody. Low and sweet the song
rang forth, as the grandmother cradled the sleeping
toddler in her arms, rocking him to and fro.

"Who is like the Lord our God," she sang, "who is enthroned on high. . . ? He raises the poor from the dust, and lifts the needy from the ash heap, to make them sit with princes, with the princes of his people. He makes the barren woman abide in the house as a joyful mother of children. Praise the Lord!"

Witnessing the old woman's serenity, Ruth almost turned to leave, rather than disturb the intimate scene. A hundred memories of her first years with the matron swept over her at the impulse, and she recalled, as if it had been yesterday, the time she had crept away from Naomi's rooftop meditation.

Smiling courageously, she stepped forward, instead of retreating, and she approached Naomi reverently.

"Mother," she whispered.

The widow started, nearly waking the child. "Oh, my dear, you are back early."

"No, Mother. I am late," Ruth laughed.

"Well," the matron shrugged, "time goes too quickly when I share it with the lad."

"He hardly shares anything this moment," Ruth teased. "He is sound asleep."

"Ah, you are wrong. Obed shares my soul," the elder corrected, "and hears my songs in his dreams."

The grandmother reached forth her arms, placing the boy in Ruth's care, and as the young woman took him, she studied the matron hesitantly.

"I could not help but overhear your prayer, just as I have done many times," she said.

"Yes," Naomi sighed. "I am too vocal with my praise."

"Not at all!" Ruth exclaimed. "But I must tell you something."

The elder listened patiently, as Ruth pursued the content of the psalm.

"So often you sing of the King in heaven," she began, "the One enthroned on high."

"Indeed. We spoke of this years ago."

"Yes," Ruth acknowledged, "but I overheard a stir in the marketplace."

"Go on." Naomi nodded.

"The people are asking for a king, a human monarch. Apparently the demand runs the length of all the provinces. What do you make of it?"

Naomi only smiled tolerantly. "Of course. This is not new. Folk in Israel frequently raise the cry for a kingdom. It is of no consequence."

"No consequence?" Ruth marveled. "The stir is very great!"

"Always it is very great, my child," she laughed.

The Moabitess was perplexed. "But just suppose," she argued, "that such a thing were to transpire. Surely, Israel will not always have judges only, and no monarch. The land is becoming too settled."

Naomi's brow was furrowed. "All right," she said, rising and pacing the court. "I will give thought to the matter. Come with me."

The boy still sleeping in her arms, Ruth followed the elder woman up the gallery stairs.

The old widow was not very strong anymore, and it took great effort for her to ascend to the rooftop.

However, when she had reached the rail over which Ruth had long ago watched Boaz, the princely horseman, the matron drew a hand across the twilight sky.

"Do you see the distant city of Melchizedek, once called Salem?" she directed.

"Certainly. Jebus. I watched it every day when I gleaned the fields."

"Its holy Mount Zion was promised to our Father Abraham."

"I recall," Ruth assured her.

"My father taught me the songs of Israel," she continued, "and one of them goes thus:

> Great is the Lord, and greatly to be praised
> In the city of our God, his holy mountain.
> Beautiful in elevation, the joy of the whole
>   earth
> Is Mount Zion in the far north,
> The city of the great King."

"Wonderful, Mother!" the girl exclaimed, her skin tingling with the lilt of the minor tune.

"More than wonderful," Naomi whispered. "A prophecy! If we are to have a king, he must reign from that noble fort."

"You have always said so." Ruth nodded, wondering at Naomi's zeal.

"Teach your son these things," the elder commanded, pointing an insistent finger toward the sleeping lad. "And his sons, as well."

The Moabitess was stone still, knowing that this injunction was of inestimable importance.

"I shall," she whispered, her eyes wide.

At this Naomi turned, taking her bent frame toward the stairs. And as Ruth watched her descend, it was with a yearning heart, and gratitude for all their years together.

EPILOGUE

I have made a covenant with my chosen;
I have sworn to David my servant,
I will establish your seed forever,
And build up your throne to all generations. Selah.

PSALM 89:3, 4
(Author's paraphrase)

When Obed had been old enough to claim his inheritance, he had decided to dwell upon the small parcel of land which bore the names of Elimelech and Mahlon.

Though Naomi had once planned to grow barley on the soil, Boaz had determined it was best suited for grazing pasture. And it was assumed that the lad would simply sell it off.

However, to everyone's surprise, the fact that the ground was unworkable discouraged Obed not at all. The lad would be a shepherd rather than choose Elimelech's art or Boaz's agrarian pursuits.

Ruth never understood her son's infatuation with sheep.

"It comes to the boy naturally," Naomi explained matter-of-factly. "Mahlon was a sheep-lover. Had he not been a potter, he would have dwelt in the hills."

The daughter did not remind her that Obed was not Mahlon's descendant. It would not have changed her mind.

And it would not have altered Obed's plans. He would be a herdsman, and so would his son, Jesse, and Jesse's youngest son, David, the light of Ruth's old age.

Thus, it had come to be that Ruth dwelt with Obed, Jesse, and Jesse's eight children in the hills beyond Bethlehem.

It had been many years since she had ventured, with her belongings, from the Ben Salmon estate, to reside in shepherd country. Naomi had long since passed away, and Boaz, too, had departed.

When Ruth had torn the neckline of her tunic and had mourned her second husband's death, Obed had sought to have her join his household.

"Mother," he implored, "it is peaceful in the mountains. There is no traffic, no bustle."

Ruth, her mellow eyes full of memory, had smiled. "You know nothing of traffic and bustle, my son."

Obed knew she spoke of Kir-Hareseth, and that her life had been a riddle of two worlds.

"It would do you good to come," he insisted.

She had never regretted her decision to abide with the shepherds. The little house, which Obed had built from round hillside stones, was a pleasant place. Its oddly positioned windows, situated to capture pastoral views down the gulleys and up the ridge, filled the shadowy interior with broad strips of light. And her own chamber, set apart by Obed, was in the quietest corner of the cottage.

By the time Jesse was past life's prime, and Obed well into gray age, Ruth, bent and frail, was the only woman in a houseful of men—ten men to be exact. Because of her age, however, she was not expected to serve them all. She cooked many a meal and mended many a torn garment. But little was asked of her.

Her favorite pastime, therefore, was to take her staff, fashioned by Obed from Lebanon cypress, and trek up the ravine behind the house. A green swatch of earth led down the eastern side to a vale from which could be glimpsed the Jordan and Transjordan.

The highway running north toward Jebus could be distinguished as it rose between folds, and her eyes often traveled to the walled city.

Through the years she had fulfilled her promise many times over that she would teach her children that Jebus belonged to Jehovah and was Melchizedek's capital. She recounted a peculiar version of Jewish history to all her young men, one in which Abraham's love for Lot and his descendants was clearly set forth.

Though she had seen the ruins of Jericho only once, on her journey from Moab, she would tell Obed, Jesse, and David that God had given Joshua strength to claim the land, and that not even the strongest walls in Canaan had kept him out.

Jesse's three eldest children, Eliab, Abinadab, and Shammah, had thrived on her tales, and were determined that when they grew up, they would be warriors.

Likely, they would one day have their dreams—for Israel was no longer governed by judges. For the first time in its history it had a ruling monarch.

Ruth had seen the years of discontent, when her adopted country continued to cry out to be like other nations. "Give us a king!" they insisted. And the elders of Judah looked to the judge, Samuel, to provide them with a royal designate.

Saul was his name. At first he had been good and just. In recent days, however, he had shown himself to be a willful man, disobedient to Jehovah.

But the hills beyond Bethlehem were largely untouched by politics. Days were quiet here, and evenings pleasant. While the youngsters of the household yearned for adventure, Ruth found herself more and more in tune with times gone by.

She knew this was the nature of very old age, to live more in the past than the present. And the serenity of the pastoral life allowed much reflection.

Her chief joy, however, lay in moments spent with the youngest of the children, for he reminded her strongly of her lost brother, Pekah.

Today, she had been sent to locate the lad, for the prophet of God, Samuel the judge, was seeking him.

She had trekked far up from Jesse's house, having left a gathering of men who had come from the village. When she had taken cane in hand and begun her search for David, Obed and Jesse had remained with Samuel and the elders around a small altar of sacrifice.

What might be the purpose of the prophet's appearance in this out-of-the-way place, she could not imagine. And no one had asked him. One by one Jesse's other seven sons had been summoned to stand before the judge, and he had, after looking at each intently, shaken his head.

He was rejecting them from some great destiny, it was apparent. But if these sturdy, capable fellows were not good enough, what use would he have for the boy David?

Even as Ruth pondered this, however, a knowing smile touched her lips. Though she could not imagine the calling which David was about to receive, she had always sensed his specialness.

Just now she rested upon the low wall of the sheepfold which marked the summit of the ridge, and faced eastward down the back side of the mountain.

Presently, she heard the tinkling of bells, and a mellow voice raised in song. She stood and began to run down the slope, waving her cane in the air.

Yes—there he was, following a small flock of sheep whose leading rams were decorated with bell-strung neckstraps. He was a capable shepherd, despite his small stature. One day he would be tall and strong as his elder brothers, but strength was not the prime requisite for this vocation.

His soothing voice, which each lamb and ewe followed, and each ram respected, often wooed the creatures with tunes of his own composition, and lyrics of his own invention. But just as often, the songs were versions of Naomi's prayers, handed down by Ruth.

"Sweet psalmist," Ruth often addressed him.

"David!" she called now.

The lad peered up the mountainside, surprised to see his great-grandmother had returned so soon. All morning they had communed together, but it was unlike her to journey this far twice in a day.

He watched with concern as she raced down the slope. "Careful, Mother Ruth!" he cried. "You'll break your neck!"

"No, son! God is with me!" she replied, coming upon him. Grasping him by the shoulders, she drew him near. "And God is with you!"

Quickly she explained her mission, and with a perplexed shake of the head, he followed after her, his eyes wide with awe.

"The Prophet Samuel?" he asked. "I have heard he is a powerful man."

"Indeed!" the great-grandmother acknowledged.

"But he has never come to Bethlehem!" David argued, panting after the one who led the way. "Slow down, Mother. You'll faint on the trail."

"God is with us!" Ruth repeated.

The way down the ridge toward Jesse's yard seemed a lifetime long. But the elder woman, supported by her great-grandson, would not turn home to rest when they reached the altar.

The lad went to his father's side and Jesse presented him to the judge. "This is my youngest son, David," he said.

Ruth stood nearby, beneath a leaning grove of palms, and listened with rapt attention as Samuel addressed the boy.

There was no mistaking the prophet's response. His stormy old eyes softened at the sight of the ruddy youngster, beautiful of face and straight as a warrior's spear.

Standing directly before him, Samuel took a small vial of oil from his own girdle. "Saul's days are numbered," the seer announced. "I have come to anoint you king over Israel."

The little congregation watched with awe as the judge raised the vial above the boy's head and let the contents spill into his curls.

"Grow in grace and knowledge, my son," the prophet instructed. "You will know when the time has come."

And then, taking his staff in hand, Samuel left the yard, followed by the silent elders.

The sun would be setting soon over Bethlehem, chased by a cool breeze off the shepherd slopes.

Ruth cared not to sleep that night. She tossed and turned upon her cot in the private corner of Jesse's house, until someone entered her chamber.

"It is I, Mother Ruth," David called.

"I know," she replied. "Come and sit with me."

"I thought you would be awake," he whispered.

"Of course. . . . "

Silence passed between them, until she took his hand.

"Remember what I have taught you," she enjoined him.

"I shall," he promised.

"Strong is the Lord of Boaz and of Mahlon . . . , " she whispered.

"And of Abraham and Lot." He repeated the catechism.

"You shall reign from Jebus," she spurred him.

"But how . . . ?"

"You will find a way," she assured him. "It is Melchizedek's city—the city of Messiah. . . . "

Suddenly Ruth's breath caught in her throat.

"What is it, Great-grandmother?" the lad asked, grasping her close.

"Oh, my son," she sighed, "I see it now!"

"See what, my lady?"

"The purpose . . . the timing . . . "

And then she was laughing softly, remembering the despair she and Naomi had often felt, the lack of understanding of Jehovah's ways.

"You are a child of Moab," she whispered.

"Yes . . . a son of Lot," he recited.

"And a son of Abraham. . . . In the end there is no

Jew or Gentile, but one people," she insisted.

"All this you have taught me."

"And Messiah shall be the Son of man."

"Yes. . . . "

"A child of Melchizedek the king. . . . "

"Yes."

"A child of the king of Israel."

"Yes."

"A child of David."

Now the boy's breath came sharply. "Mother Ruth . . . "

"It is true, my son."

David said no more, weighing the matter deeply.

Ruth lay down upon the cot, and drew the covers to her chin. "Oh, Naomi, how blind we were!" she whispered. A low chuckle escaped as she visualized Mahlon before her. "I shall never be an Israelite," she had once objected.

"Everything in its own time," he had counseled.

And then Mahlon became Boaz in her mind. "You loved a foreign woman," she whispered, "and made me a mother of Messiah."

David listened wonderingly, and tucked the widow's blankets close about her. With this she felt the glow of her husband's embrace, and sank into deep sleep.

Other Living Books Best-Sellers

ANSWERS by Josh McDowell and Don Stewart. In a question-and-answer format, the authors tackle sixty-five of the most-asked questions about the Bible, God, Jesus Christ, miracles, other religions, and creation. 07-0021-X

THE BEST OF BIBLE TRIVIA I: KINGS, CRIMINALS, SAINTS, AND SINNERS by J. Stephen Lang. A fascinating book containing over 1,500 questions and answers about the Bible arranged topically in over 50 categories. Taken from the best-selling **Complete Book of Bible Trivia.** 07-0464-9

THE CHILD WITHIN by Mari Hanes. The author shares insights she gained from God's Word during her own pregnancy. She identifies areas of stress, offers concrete data about the birth process, and points to God's sure promises that he will gently lead those that are with young. 07-0219-0

CHRISTIANITY: THE FAITH THAT MAKES SENSE by Dennis McCallum. New and inquiring Christians will find spiritual support in this readable apologetic, which presents a clear, rational defense for Christianity to those unfamiliar with the Bible. 07-0525-4

COME BEFORE WINTER AND SHARE MY HOPE by Charles R. Swindoll. A collection of brief vignettes offering hope and the assurance that adversity and despair are temporary setbacks we can overcome! 07-0477-0

THE COMPLETE GUIDE TO BIBLE VERSIONS by Philip W. Comfort. A guidebook with descriptions of all the English translations and suggestions for their use. Includes the history of biblical writings. 07-1251-X

DARE TO DISCIPLINE by James Dobson. A straightforward, plainly written discussion about building and maintaining parent/child relationships based upon love, respect, authority, and ultimate loyalty to God. 07-0522-X

DR. DOBSON ANSWERS YOUR QUESTIONS by James Dobson. In this convenient reference book, renowned author Dr. James Dobson addresses heartfelt concerns on many topics, including marital relationships, infant care, child discipline, home management, and others. 07-0580-7

Other Living Books Best-Sellers

JOHN, SON OF THUNDER by Ellen Gunderson Traylor. In this saga of adventure, romance, and discovery, travel with John—the disciple whom Jesus loved—down desert paths, through the courts of the Holy City, and to the foot of the cross as he leaves his luxury as a privileged son of Israel for the bitter hardship of his exile on Patmos. 07-1903-4

LIFE IS TREMENDOUS! by Charlie "Tremendous" Jones. Believing that enthusiasm makes the difference, Jones shows how anyone can be happy, involved, relevant, productive, healthy, and secure in the midst of a high-pressure, commercialized society. 07-2184-5

LORD, COULD YOU HURRY A LITTLE? by Ruth Harms Calkin. These prayer-poems from the heart of a godly woman trace the inner workings of the heart, following the rhythms of the day and seasons of the year with expectation and love. 07-3816-0

LORD, I KEEP RUNNING BACK TO YOU by Ruth Harms Calkin. In prayer-poems tinged with wonder, joy, humanness, and questioning, the author speaks for all of us who are groping and learning together what it means to be God's child. 07-3819-5

MORE THAN A CARPENTER by Josh McDowell. A hard-hitting book for people who are skeptical about Jesus' deity, his resurrection, and his claim on their lives. 07-4552-3

MOUNTAINS OF SPICES by Hannah Hurnard. Here is an allegory comparing the nine spices mentioned in the Song of Solomon to the nine fruits of the Spirit. A story of the glory of surrender by the author of **Hinds' Feet on High Places.** 07-4611-2

QUICK TO LISTEN, SLOW TO SPEAK by Robert E. Fisher. Families are shown how to express love to one another by developing better listening skills, finding ways to disagree without arguing, and using constructive criticism. 07-5111-6

RAINBOW COTTAGE by Grace Livingston Hill. Safe at last, Sheila tries to forget the horrors of the past, unaware that terror is about to close in on her again. 07-5731-9

Other Living Books Best-Sellers

THE SECRET OF LOVING by Josh McDowell. McDowell explores the values and qualities that will help both the single and married reader to be the right person for someone else. 07-5845-5

SUCCESS: THE GLENN BLAND METHOD by Glenn Bland. The author shows how to set goals and make plans that really work. His ingredients for success include spiritual, financial, educational, and recreational balances. 07-6689-X

WHAT WIVES WISH THEIR HUSBANDS KNEW ABOUT WOMEN by James Dobson. The best-selling author of **Dare to Discipline** and **The Strong-Willed Child** brings us this vital book that speaks to the unique emotional needs and aspirations of today's woman. An immensely practical, interesting guide. 07-7896-0

WINDOW TO MY HEART by Joy Hawkins. A collection of heartfelt poems aptly expressing common emotions and thoughts that single women of any age experience. The author's vital trust in a loving God is evident throughout. 07-7977-0

Magdalene promises hope and healing for all wounded hearts. Living Books 07-4176

Noah by Ellen Gunderson Traylor. In this imaginative novel, Traylor paints a vivid picture of the pre-Flood world in which society's tamperings with nature have abused God's creation. This story of Noah's growth and struggles is a thrilling saga of faith and courage in the face of the greatest darkness man has ever seen. Living Books 07-4699

Ruth by Ellen Gunderson Traylor. Meet Ruth, a Moabitess, as she strives to understand the people of Jehovah and finds herself slipping away from the harsh Moabite religion. Though the pain of separation and poverty would come upon her, Ruth was to become part of the very fulfillment of prophecy—and find true love on her own doorstep as well. Living Books 07-5809

Samson by Ellen Gunderson Traylor. Readers will meet the lovely, patient Marissa; the ravishing, cunning Delilah; and the friend-turned-enemy Josef. In the middle of them all is the dashing, puzzling, and romantic Samson, a man torn between cultures and two women who love him. Trade paper 75-5828

Song of Abraham by Ellen Gunderson Traylor. This richly colorful novel unfolds the tumultuous saga of one man who founded a nation. Traylor's fascinating reconstruction of the life of Abraham portrays a man of strength, will, and purpose who remains unparalleled in history. Carefully researched and superbly told. Living Books 07-6071

If you are unable to find any of these titles at your local bookstore, you may call Tyndale's toll-free number **1-800-323-9400, X-214** for ordering information. Or you may write for pricing to **Tyndale Family Products, P.O. Box 448, Wheaton, IL 60189-0448.**